FALL ON YOUR KNEES

WAYNE FISHER

ISBN-13: 978-1502882486
ISBN-10: 1502882485

CONTENTS

About The Author

Wayne Fisher lives in Garden City, Utah. After returning home from a two-year mission for The Church of Jesus Christ of Latter-day Saints, Wayne was involved in a car accident that left him unable to walk and talk. Doctors thought Wayne would never speak again. With time and effort however, some of Wayne's speech returned. Wayne painstakingly wrote this book using voice recognition on his computer. It is not uncommon for it to take him several minutes to get a single sentence written correctly. Despite these challenges, Wayne is very outgoing and shares his fun personality with everyone around him.

2 Nephi 30:4 - And then shall the remnant of our seed know concerning us, how that we came out from Jerusalem, and that they are descendants of the Jews.

2 Nephi 31:14 - But behold, my beloved brethren, thus came the voice of the Son unto me, saying: After ye have repented of your sins and witnessed unto the Father that ye are willing to keep my Commandments by the baptism of water, and have received the baptism of fire and of the Holy Ghost, and can speak with a new tongue, yea, even with the tongue of angels, and after this should deny me, it would have been better for you that ye had not known me.

Isaiah 9: 6-7 - For unto us a child is born, unto us a son is given: and the government shall be upon his shoulder: and his name shall be called Wonderful, Counsellor, The mighty God, The everlasting Father, The Prince of Peace. Of the increase of his government and peace there shall be no end, upon the throne of David, and upon his kingdom, to order it, and to establish it with judgment and with justice from henceforth even for ever. The zeal of the LORD of hosts will perform this.

Isaiah 24: 15 - Wherefore glorify ye the LORD in the fires, even the name of the LORD God of Israel in the isles of the sea.

Isaiah 44:18 - They have not known nor understood: for he hath shut their eyes that they cannot see; and their hearts, that they cannot understand.

Isaiah 45:5 - I am the Lord, and there is none else, there is no God beside me: I girded thee, though thou hast not known me.

Isaiah 45:4 - For Jacob my servant's sake, and Israel mine elect, I have even called thee by thy name: I have surnamed thee, though thou hast not known me.

Isaiah 46:1 - Hearken unto me, ye stouthearted, that are far from righteousness.

CHAPTER 1

In what is known today as the rainforest of Central America, surrounded by rich tropical vegetation, cascading waterfalls, and animals of various species, lived a young man by the name of Bartoloméo. He was the son of King Fitipaldi. He stood about six feet tall, which made him a giant among his fellow countrymen. He was about to turn sixteen—which at that time and place was a pretty big deal. He had been married for about a year and was living in his own house, right next door to his father's castle. He was pretty content with life, even though he held that his fate wasn't too fair to him, due to the fact that he was so much bigger than just about everybody else. He couldn't understand why he had been the reason behind so much snickering and teasing from his so-called buddies. This had all come to an abrupt end the day he got married.

The law of marriage was to be followed by everyone with no exclusions, especially by the lineage of royalty. It was second only to their rite of passage for males over the age of fourteen. That may seem young to you and me, but to them it was old! No one in his right mind would have allowed himself to remain a bachelor after the age of fourteen. A few waited until fifteen, but that was pushing it—at least, that was their view. Bartoloméo had a pretty difficult time trying to find a wife because of his size, meaning he had to find someone who was comparable in size and weight. However, he was very fortunate because he found one. He wasn't about to let anyone, let alone his younger—although, more attractive and athletic—brother get the better of him.

Now Bartoloméo was a second cousin to a man by the name of Nephi, who was considered to be a prophet of God by most of the people. But as has been the case in days past and present, it seemed that no one would listen to one of them, no, hardly anyone. But because Nephi lived not too far away from the old king and his household, Bartoloméo would often go listen to his second cousin twice removed—not only because they were related by birth, but because he wanted to hear "the words of a living prophet."

As Bartoloméo made his way out of the city, he tried to ignore the commotion and people running everywhere, who were currently bent on trying to keep a Lamanite from entering the city. The Lamanite had stationed himself upon the city wall in order to speak. As Bartoloméo neared the wall to exit the city—because Nephi didn't preach within the walls of Zarahemla—he happened to hear this Lamanite say his name was Samuel. Being of a curious nature, Bartoloméo thought he would stay and investigate further. It wasn't long before he was completely mesmerized.

Unless you already know the reason why the Nephites and the Lamanites weren't exactly the best of friends but were enemies by all meanings of the word, this story won't seem all that miraculous to you. If that is the case, a brief synopsis shall be provided.

The Lamanites were jealous of God's "favoritism" toward the Nephites—as they were called. Nobody seemed to know why. Becoming jealous of someone else because of something as simple as a sibling rivalry and competing for a Father's attention really is no reason to start a family squabble. However, this favoritism was only due to the very first Nephi being much more righteous than his brothers. He had proved himself more worthy than his brothers by keeping the Lord's commandments. The more righteous Nephi became, the more jealous his brothers grew, which only further hurt their standing with the Father of us all! They even tried to murder him. However, Nephi was a chosen man of God with a work to do, and they were unsuccessful. By the time Bartoloméo's story occurred, many, many years later, the Nephites were not perfectly exemplary themselves, and many of the Lamanites had become righteous. But the old hatred wasn't so easy to change.

With this history in mind, it is easy to see why having a Lamanite arrive to preach to the inhabitants of a Nephite city was not a common occurrence. As Bartoloméo was trying to leave the city, he found himself being drawn by certain words this Samuel the Lamanite was saying. So he decided he would stick around and listen. He had to return home soon anyway, because Broomhelda, his wife, was expecting him. He loved his wife dearly. She loved him, too. They were perfect for each other. He couldn't stand to be away from her, yet that seemed almost secondary to hearing from a prophet, and that's what he felt inside that this Samuel was. He just knew that some things were more important. It was a good thing he decided to stick around, too. Otherwise, there'd be no story.

"I, Samuel, a Lamanite by birth, have come to let you know of the good news. That five years hence, and the Lord Himself will come to earth in great glory: to free His people, Oh House of Israel. But because He shall be born of a woman and appear as a man, He will be judged by those in Jerusalem as a thing of naught. But behold, I give unto you a sign; for five years more cometh, and behold, then cometh the Son of God to redeem all those who shall believe on His name. And behold, this will I give unto you for a sign of His coming: for behold, there shall be great lights in Heaven, insomuch that in the night before He cometh there shall be no darkness, insomuch that it shall appear unto man as if it was day."

Samuel continued, which angered everyone—everyone that is but Bartoloméo, who was listening intently trying to pick up any catchword or phrase that might be useful to him in the future.

"Therefore, there shall be one day and a night and a day, as if it were one day and there were no night; and this shall be unto you for a sign; for ye shall know of the rising of the sun and also of its setting: therefore they shall know of a surety that there shall be two days and a night; nonetheless the night shall not be darkened; and it shall be the night before He is born."

Bartoloméo stood there in astonishment, not really knowing what he should do with all of this information. This was all new to him. He felt that maybe he should try to share it with those he loved and even with those he didn't—which weren't many. He thought he saw a good friend of his across the crowd who was also listening intently, but he didn't want to get up his hopes.

There were many who weren't so friendly toward Samuel, to whose blood Bartoloméo was ashamed to be related. These Nephites tried to shoot Samuel with their bows and arrows, but to their great surprise, Samuel seemed to be protected by an unseen force. Having seen this and recognizing it as God's power, some of them were astonished and left directly to seek out Nephi, who was baptizing in a neighboring town. But still, amidst all of this commotion, Samuel continued: "And behold, there shall a new star arise, such an one as ye never have beheld; and this also shall be a sign unto you. And behold, this is not all, there shall be many signs and wonders in heaven. And it shall come to pass that ye shall be amazed, and wonder, insomuch that ye shall fall to the earth. And it shall come to pass that whosoever shall believe on the Son of God, the same shall have everlasting life."

Samuel had said many more things, like how there would come upon the people of every land great destruction, famines, and pestilence if they did not repent. Immediately, Bartoloméo thought, *If only we were to give gifts at His birth, then perhaps my people would not be destroyed at the time He comes... And maybe, just maybe, more people will believe in Him.* Bartoloméo knew it sounded crazy. But it may just be crazy enough to work! *But first,* he decided, *I think*

I'll try my hand at getting the people here to believe. I think I'll start by telling my wife. She really is a good and faithful woman.

Over the dinner table, Bartoloméo decided to allow Broomhelda in on this new decision. He must have really struggled, because he got himself tongue-tied whenever he tried to speak to his wife. "Ere, um, I do, think, I'm pretty certain, um, no wait, I'm fairly certain, though we did discuss this when, or rather…" He hemmed and hawed some more, until, at last, "I've made up my mind to go to the land of Nehru, AND THAT'S FINAL!" He looked at her, somewhat shamefully, because he didn't want to offend her in any way and added, "of course, if that's okay with you…"

She looked at him with tear-stained eyes, and said, "Go! And I'll support you."

Next, Bartoloméo sought out Nephi in order to receive the necessary authority to begin a mission and "preach" the Word. After two days and nights of prayer, Nephi returned from his knees with the news that Bartoloméo wanted to hear: "Go amongst thy brethren."

Bartoloméo traveled a great distance, south by southwest, until he came to a land known by the name of Nehru. It was a lovely land, in its own right, but evil permeated every person, it seemed. It had become comparable with Sodom and Gomorrah. Having had no serious knowledge of the area or its people, he didn't know the trials he would face. However, he was young and foolish and strong. He was an extremely large and mighty man, so he didn't fear what any man could do to him. He had a slight knowledge of the countryside, plus he figured what he didn't know, someone in his company would. He also knew the dialect, which would come in handy for him and anyone else with whom he was traveling.

Bartoloméo began by talking to a "sea" of people here and there. Then he'd knock on doors and would start a conversation with the residents. It wasn't easy for him, but he persevered. He then decided to do some "street speeches," which were easier for him, because he could reach more people that way. He got very excited about the idea. He stood up on a tree stump that provided a good vantage point for speaking, and soon he had drawn a crowd, which only gave him more courage and bravado. He took a breath, opened his mouth, and began to be inspired: "I have traveled a great distance from the land known as Zarahemla to bring you the good news I've just heard! God, Himself, will come down and dwell with the children of men. He will be born, although He shall be born to mortal parents. He shall be known as the Son of God because He shall be conceived by the power of God, and because He shall be born to mortals. He will have the power to lay down His life, yet at the same time, He shall have power to take it up again. He shall take upon Himself the sins of the world. He shall be slain for you and me. He shall pay the fine for all of us. He shall suffer both body and spirit and be tempted above that which man can bear, except he were to die. He shall be laid in a tomb, only He won't remain there for long. For He shall be gloriously resurrected, thus opening the gateway for all of us to be resurrected, as well. We won't have to remain in these corruptible bodies for very much longer. Doesn't that make you want to shout hosannas to the highest?"

A few people he met in the streets actually invited him to dinner at their homes. He thought, *Oh great, I must be getting through to them.* However, all they really wanted... let's just say, it's not worth mentioning, but a careful study of the Old Testament will give you some insight.

In all, Bartoloméo had about as much success as the man he felt was his protégé: meaning, not that much. He could tell he wasn't cut out to be a messenger of any kind, so he set his face for home. Upon arriving, he visited his father's castle, where he found his brother, Philipiano, pacing the floors. "I'm in a worry about dad!" Philipiano complained, "Look at him! His health is not what it used to be. I fear he won't be the same with our children as he was with us! We're quite grown up, now: he just doesn't seem to have a will to live." And then he added with a huge smile, "It's probably all the peace pipes he's been smoking."

Bartoloméo replied that it was a nasty habit, and added, "Yup, them peace pipes will do it every time!"

They both had a good, heartfelt, long, badly needed laugh, which must have lasted at least five minutes. Eventually, Bartoloméo broke the laughter by telling his brother all about his experiences in the land of Nehru and how the people there rejected the gospel message he was trying to share. "I'm thinking of going to Jerusalem to witness the Savior's birth. Would you care to join me?"

Philipiano looked surprised. "What, aren't you big enough, already?" he joked. "Do you need to strike fear in the hearts of others? I mean, everyone's already pretty much afraid of you as it is: why do you feel the need to scare them more?" It was as if the world held no intrinsic value for Philipiano. He felt the world looked down on him. However, there was no justification in this line of thinking. He'd had a lot of previous success in that he could get, as it were, any friend he wanted—which, according to Bartoloméo, was quite a number of girlfriends. But this never gave Philipiano any happiness. He was always on the lookout for someone or something better. However, despite their differences, Philipiano and Bartoloméo were each other's best friend. They each had the other's back at all times.

As they continued to discuss Bartoloméo's plan, Philipiano raised an important issue: "How can you know exactly where or when the Savior will be born?"

To which, the elder of the two, replied, "True: I'm not exactly sure." Bartoloméo began to look somewhat disappointed. All of a sudden, he got this bright-eyed look on his face that seemed to say he had figured it out. "Samuel did say that there would be a sign. 'Lights in heaven'! And that the sun would not be darkened for a while. And if I were to go—I'm not saying I will or I won't—all I have to do is follow a certain star, and that will lead me right to the place where the Savior will be born! So, you see, the problem with us is that we just lack the faith to do what is in ourselves to do! If the Lord were to ask me to go to... well, any place in the world, I could!"

Sadly, Philipiano began to look somewhat doubtful at his brother, but luckily our hero wasn't that easily coaxed into believing he was mistaken. Bartoloméo continued, "I'll just have to get father to allow me the use of his boat. Tell me this, will you? What did you do when you and dad were at odds about the boat?"

A thousand and one thoughts went whirring through Philipiano's mind. Like the time he asked their dad for his permission to take his boat to see an old friend in Italy. He had been denied because the friend he'd wanted to see was considered by most to be a siren. She had the qualities of one—like the hair and the voice, but not the deadly qualities that could have gotten him killed. It was hard to convince his father of this, however, because he was so bullheaded. Philipiano wouldn't listen to the old king. He felt his father ruled out the fact that he was "of age," which to him was old (however, to you and me, not so much). Since Philipiano himself felt strong enough and old enough to go, he went anyway—much to the chagrin of his father.

Then there was the time he'd wanted to go to Switzerland to climb those really big mountains. That were considered, by most, a challenge. Once again, his father still didn't give him permission. Sure, he may have begged and pleaded with the king to allow him to go, but his father still wouldn't give his consent. He reflected back on how the conversation had gone:

"Oh, come on! It's not like I'm going to MURDER anyone!" Philipiano had protested, "so tell me precisely why it is you will not allow me to go."

"You're far too young, and that's my final decision!" Fitipaldi had become even more disturbed and red in the face than usual. He and his son were always coming to blows, especially when his second son wanted something for absolutely nothing in return.

"Oh!" Philipiano's hands began to shake uncontrollably. Beads of sweat began to form on his forehead. "C'mon, Father, you'd let Bartoloméo go in a heartbeat!"

"Yes, but Bartoloméo is much bigger, stronger, and need I mention his responsibilities? He fulfills every command I've ever given him with exactness! Shall we take a look at your track record? I believe that when it comes to fulfilling responsibilities, I've had to tell you at least two or three times as many as I've had to tell him!"

"Why won't you just admit it? You love him more! I sometimes wonder if we are even related at all! I sometimes wonder what is more important to you—me, or your precious, precious boat!" He didn't know he had become Gollum, from the Lord of the Rings.

"I said no. Can't you just let it go at that?"

Philipiano began mouthing the last words his father spoke about the boat issue. Until finally Bartoloméo began wondering what, exactly, was happening with his younger "Bother," as he so often referred to his own flesh and blood and decided to bring him back to reality. "Hello, is there anybody in there? Or are you trying to earn my nickname for you?"

"Don't ask! You might not like dad's answer." Could he have been MORE disrespectful? "But then again, you're his favorite." Philipiano began to think of something more to tell his much elder and much, much bigger brother, but nothing came to mind. "I swear, you've always—and I do mean ALWAYS—been his favorite. You could, most likely, take a boat, set off for the sunset, and no one would rat you out! I know I wouldn't!"

"You're probably right," Bartoloméo responded, feigning seriousness, "but we must always, and I do mean ALWAYS..." (He began impersonating Philipiano in every particular. He even went so far as to squint his eyes and shake his fists until he was able to get little beads of sweat to form on his forehead.) "...remember that I'm not you. I'm not about to make some huge mistake."

CHAPTER 2

Bartolomeo chose not to listen to his brother's advice and decided to seek out their father and ask him his permission anyway. As he walked to his father's throne room, he stepped into a long hallway, which to him seemed to run the whole length of the narrow neck of land on which their kingdom was situated. He passed many chandeliers and paintings on his hike to see his father. As he stopped to reignite one of the torches that had burned down to next to nothing, a thought crossed his mind: *If father doesn't give at least some of his gold and spare me the use of his boat, because I swear the man has more than one person can have, I'll be seen all around town trying to embarrass him in any way possible! In fact, I'll be very put out, so much so, he'll want to deny that we are related!* He had no idea that he was quoting a very famous modern-day novel. Yet, there were no laws of any kind against plagiarism.

Our protagonist continued to walk until he felt his legs would give out, and then he walked some more. In his hike to see his father he had passed by many, almost too many, paintings of Fitipaldi. They were actually kind of nice, he thought. Yet, at the same time, he felt his father a little too self-absorbed, a little too egocentric. However, it was good to be the son of royalty! He had no complaints.

He passed by a few paintings of King Fitipaldi watching out for his two sons: the King was waiting on shore for his two sons to finish a boat race in which he would give the victor his choice of maidens in the kingdom to wife. Bartoloméo had won that particular race that particular day, and the memory of beating his own flesh and blood made him smile.

He arrived at the last picture of King Fitipaldi giving audience to his subjects and again thought, *If father doesn't give at least some of his gold, and doesn't allow me the use of his boat...* He began mouthing the last words he had been thinking, and without even realizing, he found himself standing right in front of his father, to whom they all had to show respect.

It made Bartoloméo very nervous to be in the same country, let alone in the same room, as his father. That is how much he admired and respected the man.

Fitipaldi was sitting at his desk, pondering what to do about the kingdom. War had just broken out in many of the surrounding parts of the country. It was threatening Fitipaldi's kingdom as well. He had been going over a few strategies and ways to get the upper hand, when suddenly Bartoloméo had come bursting through the door. The king looked up at him, and with a countenance that cannot be broken by spells, no matter how strong they may be, he said, "Oh, to what do I owe the pleasure of your visit? Are you and Philipiano at it again? Because if you are, I swear..." It seemed the King had had quite enough of the two brothers' arguing over the years. It was a constant battle between them to see who, exactly, was going to be the winner at everything they tried. It was a healthy sibling rivalry, except the king couldn't stand seeing his two sons at each other's throats all the time. Bartoloméo seemed a little stunned to have arrived before his father. "I'll ask again," Fitipaldi added, "and I hate to repeat myself: is there some sort of problem between the two of you?"

Bartoloméo just stood there, believing himself to be at fault, even though he wasn't. All he wanted to do—from a troubled teenager's point of view—was to please the old king, but he just stood there and allowed his jaw to drop and his hands to shake violently and uncontrollably because of his fear of failing his father. Beads of sweat began to form on his young but receding hairline. Was there nothing he could do to make his fear of failing his father a thing of the past? To give himself at least some sort of hope in a life which was otherwise overshadowed by Philipiano?

Fitipaldi, it seemed, was being extremely patient with his son's continued silence, but even the patience of a gene code could wear thin. "What is it!?"

Finally Bartoloméo began: "Now don't become overly upset with your son, but I do have a huge favor to ask." Fitipaldi adjusted himself in his throne and remained silent, while Bartoloméo continued, "Oh, my... I don't know how to ask." He just stood on his feet, his knees buckling out from under him. He was a self-conscious individual—especially whenever he spoke to his father, the king. He decided to start at the beginning of his tale. "As I was traveling to hear Nephi preach the word of God," he began, and he then proceeded to rehearse to his father everything that had happened to him, including Samuel's prophecy, his trip to Nehru, and his experiences there. He then said, "It was all I could do, to be standing here before you, now." He then jokingly added, giving up about the best impersonation one could gave without ever seeing the movie Kindergarten Cop, yet there were only two men that size, and Bartoloméo was one of them. "Our brethren to the South lack discipline. They are soft!!" His father remained silent, so he wiped the smile off his face, which was there when he began the impersonation of Mr. Schwarzenegger. "I truly believe, Father, if we were to send gifts at the Savior's birth, many of the people we know, and so dearly love, wouldn't be destroyed as His coming... provided Samuel is correct."

Fitipaldi just leaned forward in his chair feeling somewhat doubtful about the situation in its entirety and tried not to show his disbelief—not because he didn't trust his son, but because his son had just heard a Lamanite preach what he termed "the word of God." He stood, though doing so only brought him as high as his son's shoulders, and said, "I'm not sure about all this. Why should you trust a sworn enemy? Why would you even want to trust one? He's probably making up the whole thing! My answer is a big, emphatic, NO!"

Bartoloméo looked somewhat defeated, downtrodden. "All I've ever wanted to do is please you! You know that, don't you?" He needed to say no more, only he would concede absolutely nothing to his father, this time. "You know there is absolutely no one else I respect more than you, right?"

"Okay," said a very suspicious Fitipaldi, almost as if to say, "I don't even see your point of view." "I suppose that if the sign were given," he began to snap his fingers as if to make himself think better, "you could um, uh, go. And you may even take some of my gold, too."

Bartoloméo couldn't believe his ears. He began to look around, to make sure he was the only one in the room. He discovered that he was. He felt the sun begin to smile upon him, finally. All that was missing at this point was a rainbow. The rainbow he had left out of the conversation up to this point: the rainbow of being able to borrow his father's boat to actually *get* to Jerusalem. He knew it was now or never, so he forged ahead: "All that is needed now is a mode of transportation."

Fitipaldi's eyes became fifty-cent pieces—although, back then they only had what was known as "ontis," which were most likely the equivalent. He reached up to put his arm around his own flesh and blood, and said, "You know, you really didn't have to ask my permission? You most likely could have just taken it like your brother Philipiano, and no one would have been the wiser."

With these words the clouds definitely began to dissipate in our protagonist's world, and for a brief moment he felt himself superior to his brother. What a shame it was to actually only be able to out-do his only brother in this way. In reality, Philipiano had let him win that day on the beach, because he felt that none of the many maidens in the kingdom were good enough for him. They were all much too large for his taste. Either that or they weren't spiritual enough—only it was unclear as to why he felt this way, because he wasn't all that spiritual himself. Maybe, Philipiano was just far too demanding.

CHAPTER 3

B artolomeo stepped out of his father's palace and into a warm, pleasant day. He felt a warm breeze from the ocean begin to caress his face and send a chill down his spine. He wished his wife were with him. He thought, *If only my love were here, this would be an absolutely perfect day. Oh sure, she says she's trying to make herself beautiful and proper for me, but she doesn't seem to realize that I love her already, and that there are not many things that I adore more.* He started to dance around and throw his arms in the air like Klinger from the television show M*A*S*H in the episode where Klinger had asked a girl to marry him and she had agreed, or even like a ballerina in an Opera, by Verdi. Suddenly…

"What are you doing, Bartoloméo?" Philipiano asked in a superior tone. Bartoloméo hadn't seen Philipiano standing nearby, and Philipiano could hardly resist the temptation. Even though Bartoloméo couldn't be outdone in many events, this was one time Philipiano felt he could treat their father's favorite child poorly and get away with it. "Why are you dancing around like a 'fairy young fellow'?"

"No reason. *Must* I have a reason?" Bartoloméo responded. He began to draw pictures of his wife, and himself in the dirt.

"Of course not, but it would be extremely nice to hear you admit, for the first time in your life to me, that you're an absolute failure."

"But I'm not!" Bartoloméo did another little victory dance all around his younger sibling. He became a football player who had just scored the winning touchdown in the state championship football game. "Father says I'm no longer to be in your shadow. He even gave me permission to use his boat. And I'm no longer to be envious of you! So why don't you put that in your peace pipe and smoke it!"

"But I thought peace pipes were hazardous to one's health? Just look at dad, isn't he a classic example? And do I need to stress the word 'classic' here?"

"Hey, now, that's who gave you life. And must I stress '*you*' here? Father may be older than you and me, but he's still our dad, or an abstract version thereof, and I think he deserves our complete and unwavering adherence to his rules. Not to mention our respect!" He then turned himself back to his "artwork," and continued drawing in the sand. As he drew his wife he wondered if she was missing him as much as he was missing her. He certainly hoped so. But his insecurities were soon put to rest as he remembered the last words his wife said to him as he left: "Return with honor!" Many times, in response, he'd say, "You got it, baby!"

Bartoloméo knew that Philipiano could never understand their relationship. Ever since her eyes met his for the first time, she was always trying to control Philipiano's life. What Bartoloméo and his wife had was not what would make one envious, least of all Fitipaldi's youngest son. However, Philipiano was just that. Was there nothing he could do to give himself at least a semblance of self-respect?

CHAPTER 4

T here are times such as this in a story when one must look at the whole picture and not just at the main character. One should probably do a more intense study of the supporting cast and find out what, exactly, makes them tick. In this case, that supporting cast centers around Philipiano and Bartoloméo's best friend: a man named Giovanni.

Philipiano stood about the same height as his brother, only don't ever tell Bartoloméo because he thought himself much taller than his younger sibling. Bartoloméo was so much bigger than everybody else, he couldn't be missed by many people, so he naturally considered his brother to be part of the rest of the shorter population. However, Philipiano had much more attractive features than his "much elder" (by only a little over a year, but if you were to ask Philipiano, he'd most likely lie to you) brother. But, what one was lacking in physical prowess, the other made up somehow, and in someway. They were at their best whenever they were together.

Despite their friendship, Philipiano still couldn't get over how unattractive, to him, Bartoloméo's wife was. But the one thing that really drove the man of fourteen years absolutely crazy was the way they acted whenever they were together, which was quite a bit. To him it was far too much. They were all lovey-dovey to each other almost to the point of being obnoxious. He just didn't realize that happened when a person fell in love. He had yet to experience for himself all that love had to offer.

However much Philipiano may not have enjoyed his brother's relationship with his wife, there was always hope for him to be able to find his better half. He would dream of her often, almost to the point of obsession. He tried to use every tool in his arsenal to allow himself the privilege of forgetting his brother, but there was no way Bartoloméo would give him the privilege. What did he have to do in order to have the privilege that his brother seemed to be taking for granted? Something had to change in his life, he knew that, but what could he do? It was hard to know. There was nowhere to turn. All the men he trusted were either married themselves or just trying to be jokesters—meaning they would joke about their wives in their absence, yet another trait he didn't find all too appealing. Taking advantage of about the only chance he'd get, he decided one day to take his dad's boat and set sail.

One day—deciding he was far too young to be cooped up forever by someone he viewed as a tyrant—he stormed out of his father's castle and decided to take off in his father's boat and just sail away. He thought about going to what is now Hawaii, but that was far too obvious. He also thought of going to what would someday become South Africa, but decided against it for the danger it presented—he wasn't in *that* much of a hurry to die, even though he'd made quips about his life being worthless before. Despite all of his actions, he really did care about himself, and he feared God. He just didn't show the world as much as he should have.

Philipiano stormed out of Fitipaldi's palace in a rage—he really was a hothead. Yet, as it turned out for our hero's brother, the dock was being watched by Bartoloméo's best friend, a man by the name of Giovanni. In fact, Giovanni was the very same man Bartoloméo thought he saw near the city wall the day that Samuel gave his prophecy on Christ's birth. However, there were so many different things running through Bartoloméo's mind at the time, he wouldn't have remembered seeing his friend there. It was a good thing that Giovanni had seen him that day as well, because had he not, there wouldn't be much of a story to tell.

Back on the day of Philipiano's departure, he took one good, long look around, saw no one—so he thought—guarding the boat, and decided to take it. He still wasn't sure where he would go. All he knew was that he was finally free—free to do whatever he thought he wanted. Such is the life of a son of royalty: no regard for anyone, or anything else. He couldn't wait to get out. He thought of how his dad would treat him upon his return—if he returned—and he thought of this and that and how he shouldn't even attempt to go. The thought also crossed his mind, *I bet they'll miss me while I'm gone.* The only thing on which he didn't count was how he'd feel as he realized he'd possibly seen his dad for the last time. It was as if something had turned on his own Niagara Falls, and he certainly didn't count on the taste of his own salt laden tears. It was almost too much for him to handle. However, he was a free spirit, and there was nothing that could keep him down. He'd decided that a long time ago.

In addition, because Bartoloméo's father-in-law had passed away about three years before, Philipiano and his sister-in-law had been butting heads because she was trying again and again to be left the house upon the death of Fitipaldi—which would have helped her with her dowry, which she basically didn't have due to the fact that her father had passed away long before he'd had the opportunity to give her one. All of this only caused more contention in their lives. It wasn't a pretty sight. One which you'd be glad not to know.

Grabbing the helm with his right hand, Philipiano sailed away, not caring for those whom he left behind. *It's their own fault for staying there*, he thought. After about a day's journey he found land and rested for the night to refresh himself for the next day's travel. During the night he dreamed about a man who was chasing him, and there was nothing he could do to make him stop the pursuit. The man wouldn't stop calling after him, even though he climbed a tree. Philipiano thought he recognized the man's voice as the voice of his father saying, "Come back down now! Whatever our differences are, we can work them out! Don't be thinking about jumping! You are just confused now! Won't you please come down from there? You're making your mother sick to death! Can't you see you will bring our gray hairs down to the grave?"

Philipiano awoke covered in beads of sweat. For the first time in his young life, he began to worry about someone else. Even now, it was difficult for him to acknowledge the fact that he depended so heavily on his dad. It was almost as if someone, or something, had held onto him, and—in one motion—severely whipped him into shape. He actually felt as though God, Himself, had grabbed him by the shoulders and yanked him around. Had he been with his second cousin Nephi, he might possibly have known what to do, but since he was there by himself with absolutely no help or guidance from anyone, he had to rely somewhat heavily on his own feelings. After many tears and much sorrow on his part, more than he'd like to admit, he actually received, at least he thought, inspiration from God to preach His word. He wasn't too excited about the prospect of teaching anyone. He just didn't realize, that with God all things are possible. However, he didn't feel he could baptize anyone. He felt that should be reserved for someone who had received authority from God to perform that ordinance.

CHAPTER 5

I t was a good thing Philipiano didn't win that battle with himself, because shortly thereafter, he calmed his own temper. It wasn't a very pretty sight, but one worth relating. It seems as though he didn't value the life he'd lived up to that point very much. But now, could it be probable that great things were on the horizon for him?

He decided to go out and do a little exploring. He wanted to get to know his surroundings a little better. He also felt he could use a little exercise—he was ahead of his time, being such a health-nut and all. But how else would he survive? He felt that maintaining one's health was synonymous with attracting the opposite sex, and he was known for wanting to attract the opposite sex in his hometown. Only no one knew him—or even of him—on this particular trip. For as long as possible, he wanted to keep it that way. He felt there was no need to advertise himself to anyone.

As he explored, he began to think back of Genie and of the time they had met up until the present and how she was sought after by just about every friend of his. However, he was more attracted toward blonde hair; she, of course was a brunette. She was, at the same time, a very talented singer, which seemed to attract young males from all over. It turned out, much to his own astonishment and amazement, that he'd fallen desperately in love. He even went so far as to buy her what would be the equivalent today of a promise ring, only to discover, much to his own disappointment, that she would ultimately trust someone else to be her protector. And that was all he'd wanted to do: protect her. He began thinking of the first time they had ever met.

"What's your name?" Asked Philipiano in a somewhat shy and bashful way. *A being of this high magnitude must not want to talk to me, of all people,* thought Philipiano. The smile on his face began to diminish. He felt like he was a kid, which he basically was.

"Genie," she responded. "What's yours?"

"Philipiano." He couldn't believe he was talking to an angel! Only he didn't seem to realize that angels have questions, too. Nor did he realize that angels have families of their own. He just seemed to forget one thing after another. Like how someone, so incredibly beautiful could have a mother. He did see in this new friend a lot of future potential. Despite the attraction they seemed to have to one another, he still couldn't quite get over his own insecurities. He felt like a fool whenever she was near.

"How old are you?"

He was really taken back by the question. No one had ever asked before; he felt like he needed to make himself a little older. After all, seeing no other option, there was a great need for deception; and besides, it sure was fun. "I'm almost sixteen. Just another month or two, and I'll be sixteen." Then he smiled a huge grin and said, "How old are you?"

She was completely honest with him and said she would be twelve soon, and there was no need to worry about the difference in their ages. She thought to herself, *He's a friend of a friend and that should be the end of it.* It's too bad her mom didn't really see it the way Philipiano did. Yes, just a few years and she'd become as mature as he; only he wasn't all too mature, himself.

He also couldn't keep from thinking of the time he tried to become friends with her mom—which, in his mind, was just a waste of time… They were meeting with some friends to say goodbye. They had decided to move, and there were a few neighbors that Philipiano knew, as well. It was a lovely farewell, in which Genie sang… to give them something by which to remember her. When she had finished singing, a few of the neighbors gathered around, to congratulate her on a nice job. That's all he wanted to do, too. But before he got an opportunity to even step up, her mom tried to extend a hand of friendship, to him. She said, "Hi Philipiano, I'm Genie's mom, Oxannah."

Before he could say, I know who you are. Another friend stepped forward and interrupted him. He was only able to get out, "I know…" all he could assume is that she couldn't understand him when he did that. She probably thought him far too full of himself and couldn't put himself on her level—when just the opposite was true. He actually wanted to meet her. He was looking forward to meeting her, and this was his chance. He thought she wanted the same. Only, when the other friend stepped forward, he couldn't very well ignore him as well, could he?

Philipiano emerged from his fog of memories crying profusely. He still couldn't get over his loneliness. He was trying not to miss his family, but was unsuccessful no matter how hard he tried. All he really wanted was to be loved and wanted by someone else—preferably, not a family member.

And, for some reason, he couldn't seem to find his own soul mate. *Perhaps I'll find her on this trip,* he thought to himself, but all that happened at the moment was he shed more tears.

A short while later, Philipiano wiped the tears from his eyes and became a man again. He thought himself weak because a "strong, brave, intelligent man" wouldn't show those types of things, *ever.* And he was what you would consider a tough-guy wannabe.

CHAPTER 6

As Philipiano sailed away from his rest-stop island and looked back, a strange thought crept into his mind: *What if I never make it right with dad? What if I never see ANYONE ever again? I wonder what Genie is doing right now? … I wonder if things are okay with her? … I wonder if she even misses me half as much as I do her? … I would have given ANYTHING if I could have been hers FOREVER! … Even though I say I don't miss her, I'd still like to be with her.*

Once more, he began thinking of his family and his dad: *I wonder if I can ever make things right between us? … I want to just pick him up and give him the world's biggest and best bear hug … I wonder how his health is, if it's getting any better? … I know that if I were with him, he would be doing a lot differently than he is currently … He'd probably be yelling at me, right now!* He imagined what his father would say: "What's wrong with the maidens in my kingdom? Why aren't they good enough for you? What's wrong with them?" And other questions of a similar nature. Finally he thought, *I would gladly go back, if we didn't fight so much.*

Again, his thoughts strayed to another past love. He started thinking about Cordelia, and how he really thought she was "the one" until he met Genie. In fact, quite before he had met Genie, he had been invited by Cordelia's parents to stay over for a night or two, which was a pretty big deal to them. It was also something which Genie's parents would never do! He thought, *Oh well, if they don't like me, they don't like me.* It was strange, however, because he felt he got along really well with Genie's dad, but with her mom, not so much. The reverse was true with Cordelia's parents. Only he wouldn't let his relationship with either girl's parents get in the way of his feelings toward them. Unfortunately, neither girl worked out in the end. "Oh, what am I to do?" He kept telling himself over and over again. "I need an everlasting love, not just a five minute thrill like I've been getting in the past. I need to stay in love. It's not like I can't get a smile from any girl I choose, I just would like a friend and a lover divine."

Thoughts of his mom began to enter his mind as well, how she was doing. Suddenly, the attitude of self-reliance returned to him with a vengeance. But what he failed to realize was that no girl would ever be able to replace the care he got at home—yet another fact he chose not to believe. He thought about her and her relationship with their neighbor. "How can HE do that to us? How would anyone dare oppose us? What am I doing, talking to myself in the middle of the ocean? … I don't know, she's probably going through my stuff, trying to find a mistake I may have made." Then at the top of his lungs he yelled, "You won't be able to, Mom, so FORGET IT!" He let his cowardice show, as he ducked out of the way of a flock of geese flying overhead. These birds allowed a few bombs to drop, for which he cursed them.

Despite all of these thoughts that were running through his head—thoughts that he was unloved and unappreciated—he found the strength within himself to sail on. He sailed for more than two months, though it seemed to Philipiano more like ten years. He made his way past the Iberian Peninsula, which to him seemed to be haunted. He could have sworn he heard voices.

Just to the south of Italy lies a small, (back then) uninhabited island, which is also known as Sicily. This island was unknown to the everyday traveler, for the most part, probably because of the fear that many sailors had about the Iberian Peninsula and their preferring not to die. Our present hero decided to stop for the night as he passed.

As he approached the island, Philipiano thought he could see something shimmering in the water. As he sailed over to investigate further, he noticed a shape. The shape of a woman. A beautiful woman. A gorgeous, extremely attractive, young woman. It wasn't hard for him to discern. It was as if someone had taken an angel from heaven and placed her right in the path of his boat. She was the most beautiful girl he had ever seen, with the best shape—it would easily have mesmerized any normal red-blooded male who may have happened to see her. She could have easily been mistaken for Lindsay Lohan, for she was a cross between Lindsay, Jewel Kilcher, Maggie Lawson, and Pamela Anderson—that's how absolutely stunning she was. He didn't know what to think. She was, by all meanings of the word, a goddess!

Realizing that he was in foreign waters, he felt it best to speak to her in her native tongue. Only Bartoloméo would have known this language, but thanks to his brother, Philipiano also spoke some Latin. His brother, for all intents and purposes, was the master when it came to knowing customs and languages.

"Hello, there!" he called down to her, "What are you doing in the middle of the ocean!?" From this closer vantage point, it occurred to him that she could be drowning—even though, he really didn't care about his own life, he didn't want to see another person die. His anxieties were soon put to rest, however, for no sooner had he said the words "hello there," she seemed to gain animation and brought her head above water.

"Hello yourself!" she said.

He swallowed hard and at the same time marveled that this girl would have even acknowledged his existence. He tried to be cool. He tried to seem alert and attentive to one he found so incredibly, fantastically, unbelievably, inexplicably, outrageously—and the list goes on and on—beautiful. He thought to himself, *Am I dreaming? It sounds too good to be true. To have this angel of a girl speaking to me is almost too much for me to bear. While there may be more fish in the sea, I may never get this chance again. What do I have to lose? I'll tell you what, absolutely nothing!* And so Philipiano gathered his courage and spoke again: "What's your name?

That seemed to have the desired affect. "Linda," she responded. Her name meant beautiful in Latin. "And yours?"

He had waited his entire life to see, let alone speak, to someone of this magnitude. "Philipiano!" A rush of excitement took over his entire being. He continued, "Nice day for a swim, is it not?" There had to be something more he could—and should—say, only words seemed to fail him at this time. Consider the fact that he was tongue-tied and couldn't speak anyway because of perceived loneliness on his part coupled with feelings of inadequacy, and you understand the way he felt.

"Yes it is." She was silent for a moment. She, too, saw something in him, for which she was becoming somewhat tongue-tied herself. She was falling for him. Alas, she was promised to someone else. She had to think of something quick if she wanted to be with him. But what? How was she going to be able to get her dad to change his mind about the upcoming nuptials? She couldn't very well tell her dad that she had met someone else, could she? "Care to join me?" she finally asked.

Philipiano was temped—he'd be lying if he were to tell you otherwise. "Yes..." he had to think of something great to say if he wanted to keep a friendship he hadn't even planned, which explains why he was tempted, but he also believed in remaining "chaste" before marriage. Of course, you'd be tempted, too, if someone so beautiful were to invite you to do the same. "...but sadly, I didn't bring any swimming attire."

"Well, that's all right!" She smiled. "You see, I don't have any, either."

Philipiano's thoughts had suddenly become his worst enemy. While he wanted to justify the sin—he nearly did—he also knew that God's laws are not man's laws. He thought they should get married first, but they had just met. No amount of justification could satisfy his feelings. "I'm sorry, but I believe in God, and He would be too disappointed. I will just wait for you to get dressed." She said that she believed in a supreme being too and that she understood. While she got dressed, he waited. "I don't think your dad will take too kindly to my having been here with you. What if he's so irate, and now… I hate to even imagine!"

"I don't think he will be that upset with me. He almost never is! Don't be silly." Philipiano had a slight rise of hope within. Almost as if he had just been asked to the senior prom by the homecoming queen, herself. After thinking for a moment or two, Linda added, "My dad is king of this island. You're with me. There's no need to fear… anything." And then with a burst of rebelliousness (at this moment Philipiano could see himself in her, and it both frightened him and made him dislike himself even more) she began cursing her father. "He says I'm not ever to go out. I'M TO STAY AT HOME and be PROPER!" What she said next flabbergasted him. "What do you say you and me run away together? Sure, we could just sail away in your boat. We wouldn't have to tell a single, solitary, living soul!" She tried to play to his hormones, but he seemed a little stunned. "What's the problem? You find me gorgeous, do you not?"

He thought, *How can anyone, especially the daughter of royalty, act this way?* He just couldn't see the forest for the trees. He sure was a slow learner, but, what else could be expected from one of such a high station in life? One born to privilege, only he didn't realize it. Something was definitely wrong, but if you had told him… let's just say he'd most likely have committed a very serious offense. He was about to comment when suddenly he got one of his more "normal, everyday, millions of visions." He actually got it right to demand such high expectations of this journey. He started thinking to himself, *Can I ACTUALLY BE that lucky? I must be dreaming. Quick, somebody pinch me.* Then he thought better, *I don't want to be pinched by anyone, except, of course Linda. She could, more than likely, pinch me anywhere, and I wouldn't mind.*

Linda was staring at him, much like Bartoloméo did in his father's kingdom. She was wondering if everything was all right. "Do you need help?"

"No, everything is fine. I'm all right. Thanks, though. You know, you'll make someone a terrific wife, someday."

"Why, thank you." She was, without having the slightest notion of what she was doing, making herself even more attractive to him. "I think, that's about the nicest thing anyone has ever said." Only how could she prevent him from leaving? What did she have to do to get him to stay? How could she convince him of her feelings toward him? They had only known each other, after all, a matter of minutes. Someone could have knocked her over with a feather. All of a sudden, she got an amazing, wonderful thought.

"C'mon." She grabbed Philipiano by the hand and took off running for home, with him in tow.

"Where are we going?"

"You'll see. You will see!"

CHAPTER 7

As they were running along, Linda began to explain the "rules" of the kingdom and how he should be on his best behavior—especially when talking to the king. And she told him about how fair her father was and how he'd almost never punish her for silly mistakes she may have made in the past—of which there were a lot. She respected the king far too much to ever disobey him deliberately. Even with all of this information she kept feeding him, he felt he should know more. "Tell me, how do you think your dad will react to me?"

Stopping just long enough to catch her breath she said, "I'm not too sure. But right up there, on top of the hill looking down on all, is our home. Won't you care to make his acquaintance?"

Philipiano was thinking, *Sheah, and I need a hole in my head, too.* He got up the courage to say, "On what world do you happen to be living? Your parents probably won't like me."

"Of course, they will." She said, between breaths. "Don't be silly!"

They seemed to run for miles and miles, but the entire time Philipiano was thinking to himself, *Is that a favorite expression of hers? Don't be silly. Why in the name of all that is holy, would she repeat that same phrase? And what am I doing, talking to myself, AGAIN? ESPECIALLY, in the presence of this gorgeous creature?*

Linda looked at him quizzically. She just couldn't understand how someone so refined and chiseled as he was (she saw in him everything she ever wanted in a new "friend") could be Loco. She hoped she was wrong, but she was never wrong, was she?

In a perfect world, he would've known what, exactly, she was thinking. However, since none of us lives in a perfect world—yet—he had no way of knowing. Luckily for her, he had an inclination. Of course, he would never say he had. He was beginning to think maybe he should allow his feelings to show as well.

They reached the top of a hill, and just to their right was the most beautiful castle Philipiano had ever seen—excepting, of course, his father's.

"Wow! This is the most beautiful sight I've ever seen! Again, I mean, wow! Present company excluded, of course."

Linda looked up at him, "Of course." She wasn't sure he was being truthful. She seemed very unsure of herself. She didn't know how much he truly thought that about her. And that was just how Philipiano wanted to keep it. "A few more paces, and we're there! Is there any kind of introduction you'd like?"

"Nope!" Only, the thought did cross his mind, *I wonder what would happen if I were to say, 'I'm royalty, too'? No, come on, Philipiano. May God have mercy on my soul, if I ever were to say that! You don't need the entire production of being royalty yourself!*

With that thought behind him, as well as the hundreds of other thoughts that seemed to be attacking him from all sides, he actually calmed himself quite a bit. His fears and anxieties seemed to go by the wayside. Again, he felt himself small, but in control of his life. Even the clouds of doubt in his head about the Savior—for he had many, like why he needed one in the first place—he just couldn't understand why anyone would need one, and his feelings that he was still young and foolish and needed to be taught a thing or two, began to dissipate. The well-known words of his father that would oft times reverberate in his brain came back to him: "Remember who you are, and what you love, and God loves you! And if all feels lost, you'll always have a home here!" *Strange,* Philipiano continued to think, *that he would say, 'I always have a home' when all we ever do is fight!*

Tears made it all the way down to his chin, until finally Linda asked him what, if anything, was wrong. He didn't want to show weak eyes to Linda, so instead of telling her the truth he said, "I have something in my eye, that's all." He thought for a moment, trying to gain his self-composure, and finally said, "Do you mind if we stop for a moment? I need to catch my breath, and I need someone who will accept me for who I am. Do you see any reason why your parents will accept me for who I am, and not who they want me to be?"

To which Linda responded, "I don't know why they would." She had inadvertently stumbled over some logs that were lying on the ground.

"Really!" He was dumbfounded. Philipiano couldn't believe his ears. He thought, *But I thought this one liked me.* Then he finally spoke his mind. "I can't believe this. Here, I thought we had something special."

"Oh, but we do! What I really meant to say was, WOULDN'T." She stopped running long enough to catch her breath. He stopped running, too. They just stood there, staring into each other's eyes. He felt a wave of excitement rush over his entire body. She felt the same. So playing the part of one who doesn't know anything about the laws of attraction, Philipiano brushed a hair back from her eyes, which only made her all the more attracted to him. She couldn't help herself. She wrapped him up in her arms, and leaned forward about fifty percent of the way.

He thought, *Is this girl trying to kiss me? I think all guys that know her would be jealous of me. I can't very well let this chance pass me by, can I? NO! I'd be a fool!* He felt this an opportunity to get to know this princess a little better than he already did. No words were necessary at this point. It all boiled down to feelings, and they were pretty heated and intense on both sides. He could remember what his grandfather had told him about his great uncle, and how devastated his young wife was after learning her husband had been killed, as thoughts of death seemed to surround him. No matter what he did, he just couldn't escape the ghost of his great uncle. He thought, *Oh, well, the past is the past, and there is nothing I can do to change it!*

He leaned forward the other fifty percent, and their lips met for the first time. Still wanting to get to know her a little better, he didn't dare do anything that would ruin his chances. So he mimicked her every movement, except he didn't close his eyes. He needed to say nothing, or perhaps he should have broken the silence. He couldn't understand what was happening, nor would he be able to draw on past experience that could have helped him in any way. But when he felt the probing of her tongue, he more than gladly mimicked that, too! It felt, to him, like a thousand little ants had invaded his mouth. They tickled a bit, but he knew he liked the feeling! Was it all too fast? Neither one complained! It seemed to him that the entire affair would end as abruptly as it had begun, and that worried him. He had spent his whole life in search of this girl. He couldn't very well let her go, could he? Her friends probably wouldn't have anything to do with him. Then, all of a sudden, he began to feel her hands caressing his entire body, which he also enjoyed very much. The moments with her seemed to last forever, but at the same time, they seemed to fly by. He had no way of knowing. He was enjoying himself far too much! If there were a similar feeling in the world, he didn't know.

Suddenly, a familiar voice called out on the wind to her, a voice that seemed to irritate her to no end. She really didn't get along all too well with her siblings, which would explain why she was so afraid of commitment and why she was having such a hard time with the commitment her father had made for her. Carlos made his way over to where they were, and in what sounded like an irate voice, Linda said, "What do you want, Carlitos?" Linda's little 'bother' was always getting on her nerves much the same way as Philipiano did to Bartoloméo, although neither one could comprehend why. "You'll have to excuse my little brother. He knows not to disturb me, when I'm entertaining guests."

"That's okay, Linda. I think I can be just as obnoxious as he. We all do it. Even I get on my brother's nerves at times." Flashbacks of his adolescence passed through his mind. Like the time Bartoloméo and his friend Giovanni landed on their feet—luckily—in a tight spot when they were younger. They had gone to the Iguazu Falls for Giovanni's rite of passage. Have you ever wanted to tag along with someone you admire but were denied because of perceived youthfulness and inexperience? This was exactly how Philipiano felt. He thought his chance for manhood, as seen by them, passed him like a bus that would take you to a dream job.

Carlos tried to make himself seem much larger and more important than he was. "Hi, my name is Carlos." He offered Philipiano a hand of friendship, much like Genie's mom did. He had learned from past experiences, and there was no one there to distract him. He took Carlos' hand, told him his name, and Carlos smiled a smile as big as all outdoors. It was obvious that someone needed to befriend him. He was most insecure, and that really drew him to Philipiano, for some strange reason. Linda then asked what, exactly, was the reason behind Carlos' bothering them.

"Father wants you home, now!"

She thought, *Maybe he saw the two of us together and how our bodies became one. And maybe he is irate. I really don't want to get married, especially to his choice of mates.* "Tell father I'm only going to come home if our friend here can come too!"

Philipiano started to protest, but then remembered exactly who he was and what it was he needed to be doing and finally said, "You know, I'd love to be given the opportunity to meet your father." He then added somewhat sarcastically, "I'm sure he'd be absolutely thrilled at the chance to meet me, too."

CHAPTER 8

As Philipiano was nervously waiting to meet Linda's parents, a relative of his was getting nervous as well. It seems, without him being in his father's kingdom, he had left his dad a little shorthanded. The Lamanites, many of whom were actually dissenters from the Nephites and knew of the Nephites' strategies, had decided to attack. And they were driving Fitipaldi absolutely crazy! "Why can't these people just leave us alone!? Who do they think they are, coming at us from all sides? Where is Philipiano when I need him?"

Giovanni just happened to be walking past at that precise moment. "If it will please my lord, the king," Giovanni said, "the man who finds Philipiano will be in good standing with his highness, will he not? Again, if it will please my lord, I'd like to volunteer. Given my standing with his highness and my friendship with his son, the prince, I don't want any special privileges."

The King looked at him in his usual way, which gave one the impression of being in trouble, by today's standards—but by today's standards, which are next to nothing, he would have been laughed to scorn. "But you don't even know where he is," the king protested.

"True, but I have an inkling of where he went. Hopefully, I will return with him."

Fitipaldi's eyes, once again, became ontis, "I suppose you'll want to borrow my boat, too?"

"Naturally! Of course, I wouldn't even ask if I didn't feel up to the challenge."

"You forget one simple thing. I don't even know where he went, *and* he took my boat. Even if someone did want to search for Philipiano, I wouldn't have a boat for him to do it."

"I know the king in the next kingdom, possibly as well as you. I could ask him for permission to use one of his boats. I'm not saying I could be of help in this, but I am saying I would like the chance. I was on the pier when he ran away, and I do think I know where he went. If my suspicions prove to be correct, I know where he is."

"I don't suppose you'd do me the honor of telling me exactly where he went? I wouldn't even listen to this if I felt deceived in any way." He stared at Johnny—as Giovanni was known throughout the entire kingdom—for what seemed to be hours. To Johnny however, it was only a few minutes. "You know, there's something special waiting for the one who brings back my son. It might be your choice of maidens in the kingdom to wife." The king had forgotten Johnny was already married, and therefore, wasn't in search of a wife. He suddenly realized his mistake, gained his self-composure, and giving Johnny a quick wink added, "I suppose that because of my mistake there will be untold riches for the man who brings back my son." He thought he might mention his boat, too, but then he thought he had better not say anything.

Giovanni was a very humble man, who had won the affection of his king. Therefore, he didn't feel it necessary to get more than he truly needed. He was like Bartoloméo in many respects. He would most likely just give you the shirt off his back! He had a slender build, but not so slender that he could be outdone in many events—such as wrestling and track and field. He was as quick as anyone Bartoloméo had ever seen. He was smart—as smart as anyone in Fitipaldi's kingdom. He was so brilliant, he chose law as his career. Of course, becoming a lawyer wasn't the brightest decision he could have made, but no one dared judge him.

Speaking of decisions, he was glad to have had his wife chosen for him, for she was a great support and quite a bit of help around the house. She just did anything asked of her, within reason, of course. They were best friends, which is how it should be. He failed to see the need of having an affair or being unfaithful to her for any reason. There are so many, even in today's world, who could learn a thing or two about fidelity from him.

. . . .

When Giovanni was younger, he decided to make himself a raft for his own "right of passage." Little did he know of the danger his choice of what to do for his right of passage would present. However, he wouldn't listen to anyone. Not even Bartoloméo, in his own right, could convince him otherwise.

"What, are you crazy?" Bartoloméo had said when Johnny told him his plan.

Johnny just stared at him for a little while. "What do you think I should do? Because being the best friend of royalty doesn't carry that much weight. should." and looking off to the right as some people walked past, the thought crossed his mind, *What do you guys want?* Only he didn't say it, and it was a good thing, too, because it was Nephi, the son of the prophet.

Bartoloméo could tell he'd have to do something rash if he was to keep his friend from making the biggest mistake of his life. "At least tell me where you are going!"

"And if I don't?"

"I will be forced to exercise my right as the king's son to detain you! Believe me, it's not something I want to do, but if the offender," he started quoting rules of the kingdom verbatim (not a pretty sight) "has failed to recognize any sort of authority... in this case, the best friend, or if you prefer, me... anyway, where was I?"

With his normal, agitated look in his eyes like he was being forced to do something he didn't want to do, Giovanni let out a frustrated sigh, all while doing his best to control his anger, "If you don't know, you don't know. We'll have to see if there are a few rules about not knowing. What do you say to that, Bartoloméo?"

Bartoloméo let out a mighty roar, like he was beaten at his own game and he knew it. "I'm not sure, but there are ways, and I'll find them... DON'T worry!"

"I'm sure you will." Giovanni felt the need to remind his friend that Bartoloméo was—since they were always joking around with one another— much larger than he, but then he thought of the possible repercussions. Let's just say, he had changed his mind.

Bartoloméo could tell there was no way, at least not on this earth, he was ever going to convince his friend. He had been outdone, outsmarted, humiliated in oh, so many ways. "You can do whatever you want." He said that last bit with a touch of humility in his voice. What a shame it was to Giovanni to only be able to outdo his best friend in this way. He now understood the way Bartoloméo felt whenever anyone compared him to Philipiano. "Will you at least let me know where and when?"

Giovanni just stared at his friend with another confused look. "I'll try to go against my better judgment, but it won't be easy!" He thought for a moment, then finally he invited his friend to accompany him.

CHAPTER 9

I t was about two hundred miles to where Giovanni wanted to try his luck, but this didn't deter our hero's best friend wanting to test his fate. He felt that if he was to gain the respect of their fellow countrymen, he should do something rather dangerous. So they said their goodbyes, and off they went, with a couple of cureloms—which were good for the use of man to carry necessary supplies—for Giovanni's "right of passage."

No sooner had they traveled a fair distance when suddenly Giovanni started to scream, except the scream was not one of agony. He was thrilled at the prospect of becoming a man. He actually saw the tail end of the largest river he had ever seen in his life. In anticipation of what he would be doing, they decided to hand over control of their lives to that Great Spirit— which they knew to be God, why they chose to call Him a spirit is anyone's guess! Even in today's world there are those who prefer to call Him a spirit. Could it be, because no one had ever seen Him, and since He is always fighting on the side of the right, they just called Him that out of respect? Giovanni and Bartoloméo sure thought so.

At the end of the day, they stopped to camp. Unloading one of the cureloms, Bartoloméo thought he heard a twig snap, and immediately he began to think, *Are we being followed? No, no one knows we're here. Besides, who in their right mind, would follow us?* "Giovanni, did you tell anyone about our plans for you to become a man?"

Johnny just stared, bewildered at his friend. "Why no, Bart, did you? You know, I'm getting pretty sick to death of you blaming me for anything that goes wrong!"

With Giovanni's assurance that they weren't being followed by anyone, Bartoloméo chose to go to bed. He was also extremely tired from the previous day's travel. Besides, he really was a difficult person when he was tired. Giovanni knew this to be true. He had once awoken his friend right in the middle of a "REM cycle" and soon discovered it was just best to let him sleep.

They had both failed to notice the Lamanites infiltrating their private space. There were about thirty, or so. Each one had his face painted with war paint and his head shorn to the point that Bart and John only would have seen a bunch of "skinhead O'Connor" wannabes. The two of them would have thought she has an amazing voice, but you have to admit she does come across scary looking! And that was just what the Lamanites wanted: to scare you into submission. However, one look at Bartoloméo, and they all turned tail and ran. They must have outnumbered the two of them, at the very least by 15 to 1, only they didn't count on his weight and his size. For he was much larger than anything they had ever seen in their lives. He was comparable to the mighty oak. His arms were just as big, and his legs were twice as large as anything Giovanni had ever seen. Whenever he let out a roar, either out of disappointment because he didn't get his way (which was practically never, because of his size) or out of fear (sheah… right) or whatever the reason, he was comparable with Morocco and its lions' dens.

"Eek!" shrieked Giovanni. At that, Bartoloméo came out from his tent, he was extremely irate, because he was in the middle of what he termed his "beauty" rest. Their enemies were already running for their lives and retreating to "friendlier" territory, which really disappointed Giovanni, because he thought if he could get in a fight, that would take care of his "right of passage." He, however, would still need to go through with his plans. "I really hope they try again!"

"Oh!" sighed Bartoloméo. "Do you think they'll come back for more?"

"I'm not sure, but you know Bartoloméo," all of a sudden he started to joke around, for about the third time in his life, "being with you, is always an adventure."

"Yeah, it's too bad we're so honest, or we could just tell everyone back home that you did it, that you faced your fears and conquered your demons." He then became extremely pensive, "if Philipiano had decided to tag along, he probably would have personally wet himself." They both had a good laugh, even if it was at Philipiano's expense. "It would be rather nice, wouldn't it, to tell everyone back home that you are now a man!"

"Yes, it would." He looked off into the distance, and then one can only assume he mentally envisioned his soon-to-be wife and how disappointed she'd be if ever she were to find out. "But I can't do that. It's just not me."

"But who would know? I won't tell if you don't!"

"I'm sure you won't, but it's just not who I am. It would be great! However, it's just not me."

"I understand. I mean, why should you, because of a friendship with the king's son, be allowed any special privileges? I salute your honesty." Not that Bartoloméo had to give him any special privileges, he just felt the desire to be of a more generous nature when it came to giving special treatment, especially to his best friend. It didn't take him long to realize he had just been taught a valuable lesson on integrity. Plus the fact that this all happened before Bartoloméo even met his wife and just before Giovanni and Nicole had become betrothed—for which Johnny was very grateful. However, they did know each other, and there was an attraction of sorts, but nothing was finalized until the parents gave their consent.

After thanking his friend for helping him rediscover his own affection toward his fellow man, Bartoloméo had decided to allow Giovanni to set the boat in the riverbank and see where it would take him. He was so excited, and understandably so. There was a bend in the river around which you could see absolutely nothing. The river continued to roll on peacefully, with no signs of danger; but actually there was danger: the Iguazu Falls. He had just gotten within two thousand feet when he suddenly realized it would be in his best interest to not tempt fate. Only he had decided a little too late. Going over the falls suddenly became inevitable. Death seemed imminent. When all hope seemed lost, he heard this Tarzan-like call. His eyes locked in on the source, and who did he see but this very large, giant, oak tree of a man who was bent on ruining his life.

As luck would have it, Bartoloméo had his own agenda when it came to saving someone else's life—which would explain why he wanted to go to Jerusalem. For no sooner had Giovanni heard the call than he felt himself being hoisted to safety.

When they had reached the shore and were completely and utterly safe, Bartoloméo turned to his friend, and tears started to flow. "Now, aren't you glad I decided to tag along!"

"Yeah," gasped Giovanni, "I have to admit, I am glad you came along!"

"I know, and you're welcome."

They shared a tender moment in which Giovanni thought to himself, *I sure wish Nicole were here, instead of this ugly old, oaf!* But of course, Giovanni, having accomplished his goal, finally found himself—although, not entirely, because Bartoloméo was the heir apparent to the throne—on equal footing with his best friend.

CHAPTER 10

B ack in Sicily, during Philipiano's sojourn away from home, Carlos had led Philipiano on the grand tour through his father's castle. Philipiano saw many chandeliers, which reminded him of home. He also saw many servants trying to please the king. His mind immediately wanted to cry out, *Why are you guys working and trying to please the king? Don't you know that there are better things to do? You should live in a free society, where everyone is equal! I wonder what happened, how it got to be this way? Why is it that everyone can't be like us? I wonder if they wouldn't become much-needed allies in my trying to get the king thinking this way, too? I hope Linda's family doesn't see how nervous I am. I wonder if they know, I'm royalty, too? No, I'd better not! I don't need to advertise it. They probably won't care.*

Linda caught up with them in the hallway, and after dismissing Carlos—who really didn't want to be dismissed—gave Philipiano a kiss "hello," which Philipiano more than gladly accepted. In fact, were Carlos not nearby, her kiss would have been just a little more passionate. But she felt that he would then probably run off and tell her parents, causing much more unnecessary embarrassment to Philipiano. That was something, she felt, he didn't need. "With all the attention that my family and servants have given you, you'd think you were royalty, too!"

He wanted to tell her with all his heart who, exactly, he was. But he still didn't feel the need to take advantage of his birth rite. He didn't feel it was time yet. "Some dream!" And then he added, somewhat shyly, "I think I would like to talk to your parents, if you don't mind?"

Linda, obviously, had no idea what he wanted to say to them: she just figured he wanted to ask them for their permission to take her away, which, with all her heart she wanted. He wanted the same. "You bet, mister!" she responded. The excitement in her voice would have told you more than what volumes of books could have accomplished. "Mom! Dad! ... Sorry... Mother! Father! I believe we have something that is of the utmost importance to discuss with you!"

A regular green-eyed beauty with the most exquisite features Philipiano had ever seen came into view. Next to Linda (well, there was no comparison—Linda had more amazing qualities, by far) she was the most beautiful and most attractive woman he had ever seen! And of course, right behind her was a very handsome man, in his own right. With yet another squeal of delight, because Linda couldn't wait to get out of there, she said, "I have some good news! Philipiano has a question," and then under her breath she added, "now the two of you had better like it."

Debora, Linda's mom, said, "Like what, dear?" She had fabulous hearing, almost too good.

Kenneth, her father, added, "Yeah, c'mon honey. We're dying here!" He then flashed a smile as big as his son's. "Out with it!"

Biting her lip, Linda began: "I think Philipiano has something to ask you."

Philipiano felt his knees begin to buckle. He didn't know why, but it was just like when he met Linda for the first time. He was just as nervous this time, but you'd never have known he was nervous when he met Linda, because with her he was trying to be as debonair as possible. He felt he had to come out of it but didn't know how. He was tongue-tied. He had never, even before in his life, felt the pressure of having to speak on the ways he and his family lived, nor about what they believed! He thought, *Where is Bartoloméo, when you need him?*

"My brother is definitely better at this than I. But since he isn't here," and then he added under his breath much like Linda did before, "and is probably glad to not be here!" It seems, Philipiano had forgotten about Debora's enhanced auditory nerves. Immediately, he turned back to face them, because he had been looking away ever since he had said that bit about his brother. Without further ado he asked, "Do you believe in God?"

They all began to fidget nervously in their chairs—including Linda, who was looking somewhat disturbed that the question wasn't directed toward her going away. But Kenneth spoke first, "I am afraid I don't know what you mean."

"Do you believe in a Great Spirit? An all-powerful being who controls the universe?" If this is beginning to sound familiar to you—and hopefully, it is—that's because Philipiano had a close friend who was the great-nephew of Aaron, Omner, Himni, and Ammon, who happened to be some of the greatest missionaries of the Book of Mormon. If you don't know the history, then by all means, talk to a pair of missionaries from The Church of Jesus Christ of Latter-day Saints, they'll know what to do. Philipiano continued, after what seemed to be a chorus of agreements. Without even knowing, he began imitating Bartoloméo—just don't ever say anything of the sort to him, please.

Linda had decided to speak up for herself. "But I thought…"

"All in good time, Linda." Philipiano said. "The only problem with asking them is that I'm not sure they'll want you to go." She started to tear up, until Philipiano put his arm around her and tried to console her.

It seems that both Linda and Philipiano had temporarily forgotten what marvelous hearing her mother had. "All in good time, for what?" Deborah eyed him somewhat suspiciously, because she really didn't want to lose her youngest daughter. She began to grow somewhat uneasy, making everyone in the room uncomfortable as well! "Where wouldn't we want her to go?" And with a glare that could kill she added, "WELL, I'm WAITING!"

Philipiano swallowed hard, trying to skirt the subject. He thought to himself, *Wow, could this be as hard as they are making it?* "I think, maybe, Linda should tell you." His eyes darted back and forth, until he reached Kenneth. "Don't you think?"

"Yes, she should," he said, while glaring at her with a look that would make your hair stand on end.

Debora too, gave her daughter a nasty look which spoke volumes beyond anything Philipiano had ever seen—nor did he ever want to experience anything of a similar nature. But she spoke anyway, "I think, our guest should do some talking for himself! I'm just spit-balling, and if anyone could give me some support here, KENNETH!" She turned her gaze from her daughter back to her husband.

"Anyway, as I was saying," Philipiano turned his focus back to where it should have been at all times: toward Debora and Kenneth, even though he would have preferred to give it all to Linda. "This Great Spirit is also known as God. He is in all things. He is aware of everyone of us!" And then he tried telling them about the heavens and how God dwells in them, as well as in our hearts, which is why we have to keep ourselves in the best physical condition as possible, meaning we shouldn't do drugs, have premarital sex, drink alcohol, and definitely shouldn't smoke, all while trying to maintain ourselves in optimal health. These are pretty strict guidelines, but they won't kill you! In fact, they'll only make you healthy and strong. They are for your good!

Philipiano tried a totally different approach, "When you look at the world, what do you see?"

Kenneth answered, "I'm not sure, exactly, what I see. However, I believe there are things that can bring us to our knees."

Philipiano told him—actually, told them all—that he was right. That if everyone in the world would just believe that too, the world would be a much better place to live. But it has to start at home. We can't just have others do that which we can do ourselves.

Before long, Deborah decided that Philipiano was right, that what he said actually made sense. Kenneth too, felt something within himself—something he had never felt before. He asked why he felt this way, what these feelings were, and what he needed to do to have them with him always. Philipiano told him that it was a spiritual bond between him and the Lord, and if he wanted to keep these feelings from ever leaving him, all he had to do was to get on his knees and truly humble himself, and he would feel and know things which are indescribable.

They both did just that, and they discovered that God does live and loves us! How it was discovered, while not a secret, is something of a spiritual nature. After seeing how much Philipiano loved her parents—because of his concern for their salvation and his love toward them all—Linda, too, became converted, as did her brother, Carlos.

Later that night, Philipiano found himself walking through the palace garden, mentally reviewing the day and what had transpired. He felt pretty sure of himself. Linda decided to join him after seeing him in the garden all alone.

"I think one needs to be more than alone, don't you? Especially after the way you spoke to my parents. I think that deserves a celebration." Trying to be as coquettish as possible, while trying to keep herself pure and chaste at the same time, she wrapped him up in her arms again.

He started to feel Linda's passion again, when all of a sudden he saw something else in the water. His thoughts immediately flashed back to happier times. Only he wasn't too thrilled this time, even though, he was so enamored with Linda. He recognized the boat as his dad's neighbor's and immediately thought, *Why does he insist on ruining my life? I'd like to know how he found me!* He finally broke the silence and spoke his thoughts aloud, "How in the world did he find me?"

"Who?" inquired a very frustrated Linda.

"My father," replied an even more frustrated Philipiano. "He is just too much of a busybody to become part of my life. He just doesn't know when to leave well enough alone! I'm not too certain, but I'm almost sure he is in the boat!" And then with a moan of disgust, "Arrgh!"

CHAPTER 11

Philipiano did not enjoy his life at this moment. He thought, *Why is he following me? How did he even know I was here? What must I do in order to gain freedom from the oppression known as Fitipaldi?* He made the mistake of telling Linda, "My father is relentless."

Linda said, "Let's run away! He doesn't know you're here, does he?" In response, Philipiano just shrugged his shoulders. "But he can't know! It just isn't fair!" She broke down in a flood of tears, and gazing skyward while shaking her fist, "You hear me? It's not right!"

Philipiano was feeling the same way. "What, did he never have a life of his own?" He was becoming even more attractive to Linda. She was frightened and aroused at the same time. Can you blame her? She felt she was waging a losing battle—one she wasn't sure she could win. Nor did Philipiano try to help her win. It was difficult for her to know where he stood, because he stated to her all the time that he wanted to stay, but in the end when it came down to knowing exactly what he would do, even he didn't know. He was far too wishy-washy.

"Oh well, all good things must come to an end, I suppose. But why can't we just go away together? He'll never find us! Just do me a favor, and don't ever forget me," she said, while trying to be as brave as humanly possible. Also, she had thought of a trick she had learned from her mother, and it seemed to work whenever she wanted anything from her dad. It always worked on Kenneth whenever Debora wanted something that otherwise she couldn't have. She would just bat her eyes at him and he'd be putty in her hands. Philipiano, however, had more inner strength than his alter ego, Kenneth. And for that, he was glad. Of course, the island life wasn't all that bad for Linda, either. She craved adventure! Heaven knows just how much she wanted him to take her away, and it also knows just how attracted they had both become to each other. It was Bartoloméo and his wife all over again, but Philipiano would beg you to not ever tell either one!

"No. He's relentless. He'll stop at nothing. I am his son. Perhaps things have changed in the kingdom." Realizing he had no other choice he added, "I may as well go. He'll find me no matter where I am." He let out yet another groan of frustration. "I really shouldn't go! Can I stay here with you?" Linda got this wide-eyed look that Philipiano was hoping she'd get, because he really wanted to stay, but he thought better of the situation. "When your dad gets mad at you, what do you do? I mean, do you run away? Ever? No!?" He looked at her, bewildered: he couldn't leave without her, could he? He just felt too much of an attraction. However, he also knew that back home he had responsibilities. He envisioned the Lamanites attacking his dad's kingdom and how much his dad needed him. He thought to have seen his dad crying, which just about broke his heart. "No, I better go. I think my dad needs my help." And with a very sorrowful look in his eye he said, "It's time I stop making him chase me all over the world and became a man." Little did he realize that in order to become a man he had to first act like one and tell them who, exactly, he was.

Linda had excellent auditory nerves like her mother. "I won't let that be! Not for all the money in the world!"

"Thank you!" He took her in his arms, hanging onto our present heroine ever so passionately, "I wish I could take you with me. I should have said so from the beginning and not gotten our hopes up, but I can't do that to your betrothed. If he is married to you, I agree that he would be the happiest man on this planet, and I couldn't do that to him, even though I don't really know him... I could never..." Being so softhearted himself—almost to a fault—he broke down in a flood of tears. He had forgotten he didn't want to show weak eyes to Linda. But what else could he do? He was trapped, and he knew it.

Linda, however, failed to notice that he had inferred that his father was a king, which made him royalty, too.

She was too preoccupied and self-absorbed with the fact that she was not going to get off the island. She was still in denial, and had her head so far in the clouds. She was head over heels in love with Philipiano. And rightfully so! Not only had he become her hero, he had also become her best friend in the time they had spent with each other. She felt like she could tell him anything, and she did! If he had just told her who he was when they had met; things would have been a lot different.

Before long, Kenneth came out to bring them a message. With tear filled eyes—because he felt he wanted Philipiano to stay as well—he said, "I have something to say. I have a message for Philipiano that I'm afraid he would rather not get." It had completely slipped Philipiano's mind to tell them all that perhaps his father might come looking for him. It had just never crossed his mind that just maybe his dad had dared look for him. Fitipaldi was scared to death of the ocean—he had lost a very close relative to the sea when he was young. "Your friend, Giovanni, has come to get you. I've just spent the past hour trying to talk him out of taking you away."

"Giovanni!? Really? That's a surprise! I thought for sure, my dad would have been the one to come and get me." The look of worry that had been on his face was suddenly replaced by relief. Kind of like when you think you're in trouble and come to find out the price for your transgressions and sins has already been paid. This is true in yours, and my life, too. Won't it be nice when we all are resurrected, because of Jesus Christ and what He has done for us? However, just because He has died and paid the ultimate sacrifice on our behalf, that doesn't mean we can just do what we want. We have to keep His commandments, which really aren't all that hard, but "a religion that doesn't require the sacrifice of all things, never had the power to save (a soul)." And you can see the effect of what total sacrifice of those whose hearts are truly contrite and penitent can have: they have a profound influence on the world!

At that precise moment in time, Giovanni decided to let his presence be known. "Philipiano!"

"I could recognize that voice from anywhere!" Philipiano responded. With a wide-eyed look, he continued, "What brings you here? I thought for sure, you were my dad! I'm glad to see you! I'm so glad you came and not him." Then facing Kenneth and Linda he explained, "This is Giovanni. I think he has come to take me back home. Little does he know, I don't want to go back home with him." Then under his breath, because he had temporarily forgotten what good ears Debora and Linda had, and he only could assume Kenneth had them as well, he added, "I would give anything if I could stay here. I don't want to go. I'd rather stay!" Then he turned his focus to where he didn't want—Giovanni. "I was surprised to see you here. I wish you could see how much I love it here and how well I am treated." He was basically treated as though he were a god. It was easy for one to discern why he wanted to stay. He felt at home with these people. Why would anyone, in his right mind, want to leave? He had only been there for about a year and a half, or so, but he felt so good—almost as if it were his second home.

"It's time to go, Phil!" Linda's family didn't know Philipiano's nickname back home. The chance to tell them had never come up.

They started to tease him like never before. Kenneth began singing, "Is it time to call right out and end our friendship?" He was always making up songs. He had a kind of talent to sing whatever song he wanted, at will. That was one of the things Philipiano wouldn't miss about the island. On the other hand, there was one thing he would miss, and she stood about five feet, seven inches tall, had the most gorgeous eyes and blonde hair he had ever seen, not to mention the most incredible body. She had taught him a thing or two about how to treat someone about whom you can only dream.

The sun was rising over the ocean, causing Philipiano's dream to be short lived because he had to return with Giovanni, which he was quite certain he didn't want to do. However the sun began shooting forth freely its relentless rays and causing a sparkle that can only be equaled by your imagination, while at the same time, becoming his worst enemy.

Giovanni could see why the king's son didn't want to return with him. "One look in those gorgeous green eyes, and I would have become her slave! And no, I'm not saying I would be hers for just a day, but forever!" Philipiano, however, could see it in Giovanni's eyes that he wasn't being quite honest with himself, because he was far too in love with Nicole.

"I know, I know! Why do you think it was taking me such a long time to come home?"

CHAPTER 12

At the same time as when Giovanni reached the shores of Sicily, Bartoloméo was having his own problems with the Lamanites. His best friend had gone, leaving him desperate against their enemies. He thought, *How come I have to stay, and Giovanni and Philipiano don't? Do you ever wonder how I would be if only they were here!* He let out a groan of frustration toward his best friend and his brother. Not a pretty sight! Of course, nothing about him was remotely attractive, except maybe his sense of humor—of that there could be no equal.

He was, on the other hand, an extremely large man in the eyes of his enemies, which was good enough for the king, who was so very happy that Giovanni was probably—supposedly, hopefully—in search of his other son. This, obviously, was driving Bartoloméo absolutely crazy—because he wanted to be the outright favorite.

They saw each other in Fitipaldi's super long hallway, and Bartoloméo tried his best to extract information from the king, "Oh, come on, father. Where did they go? I know you know! You're going to have to tell me sooner or later!"

"I don't see how you need to know!" Fitipaldi did not like to explain himself. "I don't like it very much when I need to repeat myself over and over! I feel like I'm a parent of a brand-new baby! Like I did when you were born. Either that, or take your pick of any one of your siblings. In my opinion, you were all so cute." He stopped, gathered his thoughts, and it seemed to Bartoloméo he had become somewhat sad and disappointed; because he felt himself a failure! Every one of his kids, even Philipiano—although they did butt heads on occasion—still respected and loved their dad with all their heart! "I just wanted to pick you up and eat you all on the spot. Then I formed each one of you as best I could, trying to give you the best head start possible… and you all turned on me by becoming teenagers. I found that none of you came with a 'return to sender' attached.

"What was I to do? I couldn't very well have turned you out on the street, could I have? I didn't think so! Here you were, helpless, harmless little tiny bundles of joy, as *infants*," he emphasized the word infants and continued, "then it hit. What I like to call the terror of teenage years! Your brother has yet to outgrow it."

Bartoloméo began to snicker at how his father had made fun of his younger sibling. Of course, it was easy for him to be their dad's favorite at that time, because he was there! No matter how much Fitipaldi seemed to be favoring his eldest son, he really did love them all the same. He just favored Bartoloméo because the elder of the two was just a little more obedient!

Much to his son's bewilderment and disappointment, the king continued, "But you, on the other hand, are the eldest son, and as such have responsibilities. Not only as my son and having been born to such great privilege, but also having been born to the special privileges that only come on account of being royalty yourself." The look of fear and confusion on Bartoloméo's face spoke volumes. "You've got to comport yourself in a way that will reflect nothing but good on your old man." Fitipaldi said that bit about being his old man behind a smile. "Although you don't realize this, your brother does look up to you! In fact, he wants only to do that which you can't."

Bartoloméo began to protest, and before he could get out a single word Fitipaldi cut him short by raising a hand in the air. "Now just hold your horses! Be patient! I'll figure it out. Now, where was I? Oh yeah, I remember. You mean to tell me, you don't know that your brother looks up to you? Well, he does. Before he left (only goodness knows where he went) he told me he wanted to be just like you when he is older—'much older,' is what he said. I guess we'll have to wait and see. Hopefully, Giovanni will find him. You know, a lot has been said about your best friend. Now we just have to wait and see if he can measure up to all the hype." Without even realizing what he had said, these words told his eldest son everything... well, almost everything! He just had to get his dad to tell him where his friend had gone. However, the king had no idea himself. That was how far out of the loop the king was.

Bartoloméo was every bit as smart as his friend, and while not the best apple in the bunch (especially if you wanted to field a sports team), he could tell you your innermost thoughts. Therefore, he knew his father's thoughts, which could either be bad or good depending on whether or not he liked you. That was how close Bartoloméo tried to live to the spirit of our Heavenly Father. He was always helping out and trying to serve his fellow man. Yet another reason he was in such good standing with everyone he met. His service to his fellow man didn't hurt his relationship with God, either. He was always on the lookout for a chance to serve, and these chances were all around him.

Absolutely no one was daring enough to take on the king or even his wife. Bartoloméo just couldn't understand why anyone would want to encourage that type of living. Of course being of royal lineage himself, he had no idea of what it was like to be poor. He just couldn't understand, or refused to learn, what it is like to beg for your next meal. But then again, neither did Philipiano, who was also of the same mindset. However, they had both developed a certain "savoir faire" when it came to knowing what to do and what to say.

Only Fitipaldi truly understood what it was like to be poor. He had become known for his great strength as a boy, which only helped him in his quest to become king of the land. Of course, he drilled in his children a sense of fairness toward the less fortunate, which they more than gladly took to heart. Not one of them was lazy or slothful in any way, which only made the king even more proud.

Despite being proud of his kids, to whom Fitipaldi referred as the joy of his existence, they still kept him out of the loop when it came to knowing what to do, what to say, how to act, etc. However, there was one thing he knew beyond a shadow of a doubt: he absolutely loved and trusted his son far too much to dismiss Bartoloméo's belief in "the Son of God." He went over again and again the evidence of the past few days and how many of the signs of the prophets were beginning to be fulfilled. "Nevertheless, the people began to harden their hearts, all save it were the most believing part of them, both of the Nephites and also of the Lamanites, and began to depend upon their own strength and upon their own wisdom, saying Some things they may have guessed right, among so many: but behold, we know that all these great and marvelous works cannot come to pass, of which has been spoken.

"But behold, we know that this is a wicked tradition, which has been handed down unto us by our fathers, to cause us that we should believe in some great and marvelous thing which should come to pass, but not among us, but in a land which is far distant, a land which we know not; therefore they can keep us in ignorance, for we cannot witness with our own eyes that they are true.

"And they will, by the cunning and the mysterious arts of the evil one, work some great mystery which we cannot understand, which will keep us down to be servants to their words, and also servants unto them; for we depend upon them to teach us the word; and thus will they keep us in ignorance if we will yield ourselves unto them, all the days of our lives."

Even with all of this easy-to-see evidence that would cause the hardest of hearts and the most unbelieving of all men to believe, the king still had a hard time. Which, if you think about it, you and I would have had the same hard time. Because each one of us needs to have faith in Him, who we haven't seen either, as far as we can remember. "Well, let's hope for your brother's sake that Giovanni can track him down!"

Bartoloméo's hair on his young, but receding hairline, stood on end. That was how much he respected, and feared his father. "God, I hope so."

Fitipaldi just stared, flabbergasted, at his son; "I hope you're aware of what you just did!"

Without even realizing it, Bartoloméo had just taken the Lord's name in vain—sound familiar? Far too many of us are not aware of how we take the name of Deity on our lips. However, once Bartoloméo realized what he had done, he fell to his knees and asked forgiveness! "Oh, dear father, I'm so sorry! I promise that I shall never, ever take thy name in vain again."

Of course, his love for the Savior never diminished. However, he did miss out on a few blessings he could have otherwise had. Directing himself toward the king—who, at this point wasn't so sure he would allow his son to take his boat—Bartoloméo said, "I sure hope he finds him, too." He sheepishly asked the next question. "Even if Giovanni doesn't return with your boat, would you still be willing to allow me to go?"

"I'm not even sure you can be trusted, taking The Lord's name in vain like that. I'll have to think about it." Fitipaldi added, behind a smile, "Besides, if he doesn't return, I'll have no boat to lend you. Even though I shouldn't doubt, I do."

"Don't lose faith in Giovanni. I'm sure you'll see your boat again!"

"Do you really think so? I wish I had your faith! I've just been informed by our spies that the Lamanites are not threatening to attack any more, so that's good news. I suppose it would be too much to ask for more good news." Then he added under his breath, because he was ashamed to admit he didn't trust his son's friend as much as Bartoloméo did, "Like, if Giovanni would return with my other son." Without even realizing what he had done, Fitipaldi had just made fun of himself, because he too had imitated Bartoloméo.

This, of course, forced a smile across Bartoloméo's face, which the king, for some inexplicable reason, didn't understand, and there was only one reason for which his eldest son would explain it to him. But he'd already received permission to go, so there was no need. Instead, he respectfully—although, with a smile—said, "Not to worry, father. Giovanni wouldn't deliberately disobey you." And looking off toward the distance, he added, "Not if he knows what's good for him!"

Later that night, Fitipaldi noticed something. It was something he had never seen before, nor did he think anything similar would ever happen. He noticed the sun going down, but the sky didn't get dark as it had on every other night of his life.

"And there were many, who had not believed the words of the prophets, who fell to the earth and became as if they were dead, for they knew that the great plan of destruction which they had laid for those who believed in the words of the prophets had been frustrated; for the sign which had been given was already at hand.

"And they began to know that the Son of God must shortly appear; yea, in fine, all the people upon the face of the whole earth from the west to the east, both in the land north and in the land south, were so exceedingly astonished that they fell to the earth.

"For they knew that the prophets had testified of these things for many years, and that the sign which had been given was already at hand; and they began to fear because of their iniquity and their unbelief."

Doesn't that make you wonder why no one will listen to the prophets today, and get a year's supply of food, just in case. Bartoloméo would bet his own life, the people in the Philippines, if they could, would give anything to have the opportunity!

"And it came to pass that there was no darkness in all that night, but it was as light as though it was mid-day. And it came to pass that the sun did rise in the morning again, according to its proper order; and they knew that it was the day that the Lord should be born, because of the sign which had been given.

"And it had come to pass, yea all things, every whit, according to the words of the prophets.

"And it came to pass also that a new star did appear, according to the word.

"And it came to pass that from this time forth there began to be lyings sent forth among the people by Satan, to harden their hearts, to the intent that they might not believe in those signs and wonders which they had seen; but notwithstanding these lyings and deceivings the more part of the people did believe, and were converted unto the Lord.

"And it came to pass that Nephi went forth among the people, and also many others, baptizing unto repentance, in the which there was a great remission of sins. And thus the people began again to have peace in the land."

Fitipaldi could have sworn he heard shouting emanating from Bartoloméo's home: "Yahoo! It's the sign! The Savior of the earth is being born! I knew we would be freed from Satan's grasp!"

CHAPTER 13

The previous night, as Giovanni lay awake, listening to the crickets just outside the window of where he would spend the night, a terrorizing thought came to mind, *What if Samuel is mistaken? I mean, there is no doubt in my mind that a savior WILL come. I just wonder if He will come as Samuel says? Strange, that He would be born in the flesh, and somewhere far away. It seems to me that he is just too old, but you never know. Stranger things have been known to happen! And, a virgin? It all seems pretty unbelievable to me! Plus, if I don't believe, how can anyone else? I'd say, even though Samuel is nothing more than a Lamanite, which is why we shouldn't trust him in the first place, I owe it to Bartoloméo to give him the benefit of a doubt.*

In order to be on the safe side, no one felt it more necessary to believe than Giovanni. Which meant he had to let go of his trying to prove the prophets and their promises false.

At that time, who would come into the room but Philipiano. "How are they treating you?" he asked, somewhat hopefully. He wanted to make everyone around him as comfortable as possible. He was like his brother in that respect.

"Pretty well, I suppose. Only, tell me this, do they treat you as if they knew you were royalty yourself?"

"Yeah, why?"

"No reason." Giovanni felt himself much too small in comparison, but he would never tell another living human being. "I'm just not comfortable with it, that's all. Of course, not being royalty myself, I've gotten used to being mistreated in your father's kingdom. So why should it be any different here?"

"You want to know? I'll tell you why! Because no one here knows who I am. I'd kind of like to keep it that way, if you don't mind?"

"But why? If I were you, I'd try to tell everyone! I mean, you don't seem to understand the power you can have, being of such high birth. I, personally, don't think you realize the great potential you have!" Finally, pulling himself out of his own pity party for not being more of an upper-class and elite person himself, he added, "Why won't you realize your potential? Sometimes I'd like to pick you up by the ears and just throw you around!"

This caused a smile to cross Philipiano's lips, and he began to chuckle inwardly. However, he maintained his silence, which was probably a good thing for someone in Giovanni's state of mind. He now wished he hadn't semi-volunteered for this trip, let alone "reprimanded" his best friend's only brother.

"I'm sorry! I should never have spoken to you like that!"

Shocked doesn't begin to describe Philipiano's feelings at this time. He thought everyone in the kingdom was aware of his feelings toward being of noble birth. "You can't just pretend, now can you, that I'm not royalty?"

"I am not sure. I don't wish to misrepresent myself to anyone. Besides, it's not in harmony with keeping the commandments. And I hate to disappoint you, but I fear God even more than I do you." He had forgotten, temporarily, one of God's laws: to make himself subject to the laws of the land, in other words, not to doubt in the king's son. However, Philipiano himself wasn't about to tell anyone. That was how disgusted he was at the prospect of becoming king, which would happen if (and that's a big 'if') his brother had in some way refused the kingdom. There was absolutely no way Bartoloméo would have given up the kingdom willingly! Besides, there was no way, at least not on this earth, his wife would allow that to happen!

Giovanni continued, "I do fear you, but in your case more out of what you can do to my physical body. As such, when God commands, I obey because I love Him, not because I'm afraid of anything He may, or may not, be able to do to me. Not that He can't, I just don't think He will. I'm sure He has wanted, various times in my life, to just strike me down! I'm certain, the same could be said for anyone on this planet. But thanks to the One for whom we are waiting, and His atonement, we all can improve. That is why, I believe, your dad needs his boat to loan to Bartoloméo, so he can go to the land of our nativity, to try to witness the Savior's birth. You know, there are those who say He won't be born, but not my best friend. You know he has more faith than anyone I've ever seen!"

Philipiano raised his hand in agreement, but Giovanni thought he was a dead man because of the way he had spoken to the son of the king. However, Philipiano had always been taught to follow the 'golden rule,' meaning he wouldn't take advantage of his bloodline. Needless to say, their friendship grew by leaps and bounds that day. Giovanni decided that he would defend the kingdom at the expense of his own life, or rather he had already made the commitment many years before, but this just felt like a good time to renew that covenant. "I swear that I shall defend the kingdom, or anyone therein, with my own life, if necessary."

"I'm sure you will. I don't see anyone in the kingdom who is more faithful to us than you are." When looking out the window, he noticed something. Something around all that seemed to penetrate to his very core. The sun was going down, but the sky failed to get obscure. "Giovanni," he asked, "on which side of the earth does the sun set normally?"

"Generally, the west. Why?"

"No reason. It just seems strange that something I've seen time and time again would be playing tricks on me!" He had forgotten the reason he had to return home, the reason Giovanni had come looking for him in the first place. Why Bartoloméo needed the boat, and so on. "There are strange goings-on afoot here." Could it be, he just didn't want to leave in the first place? He was having too much fun with Linda; and she, most definitely didn't want him to leave, either. He knew deep in his heart he had to return with Giovanni. Yet, how many of us would choose to follow our heart, instead of choosing the Savior himself? His plan is so much better than anything we could imagine. But He doesn't want us to believe on miracles alone, He wants faith on our part!

Philipiano couldn't believe what he saw next. As he turned to face his brother's best friend, he noticed Giovanni wasn't as tall as he usually was— he had fallen to his knees. Philipiano immediately thought, I had better follow suit!

Linda came walking in, "Hey guys, do you know what's going on outside?"

Of course, no one spoke a word. Philipiano motioned for her to get on her knees, which she did. They knelt for hours, no one speaking a word. Suddenly, Carlos appeared out of nowhere, his dad and mom with him. They, too, began to question out loud what was happening. They couldn't understand. After about a minute of questioning and not getting an answer from anyone, they fell to their knees as well; apparently, they were also afraid of this mystery that seemed to have paralyzed their guests and their daughter, too.

Giovanni looked up at them all, and in a voice which was full of excitement said, "It's the sign which we have been promised, and for which we are waiting and longing. It's the Son of God! He has finally come!" He then rose from his knees and started jumping for joy with a countenance full of surprise and wonder. "I can't believe I get to witness this! How fortunate am I! I thought, for sure, the sign would only be given at home! But I suppose, and believe, God is no respecter of persons. I am now completely positive that He loves all His children everywhere! It doesn't matter if you're rich or poor, black or white, bond or free, educated or ignorant. It just doesn't matter! Now, we are all made equal in His sight!" He then turned to face his friend, who, by the way, was still on his knees and crying due to his unbelieving and doubtful heart. He, himself, still needed to understand some things.

Possibly Philipiano needed to strengthen his own testimony. Or could it be, he was going to be a man soon and in order to be better qualified for this he knew deep in his heart that he couldn't rely so heavily on his brother's testimony? Nor could he continue being so "spoiled" as far as his dad was concerned—he'd have to earn his own way. He wasn't too thrilled at the prospect, not that he was lazy, or anything, but being the man of the house actually scared him. He wasn't sure he could measure up to his dad. Then again, not too many people could even be in the same category as his dad; that was the kind of man Fitipaldi was.

CHAPTER 14

After the "night of surprise and wonder," Philipiano, Giovanni, Linda, and her family all gathered on the dock by the ocean. No one spoke a single word. They were all much too flabbergasted at what had happened the previous day. It was all unexpected. So unexpected that they just stood there, staring at the water and all the fishes and other forms of sea life who were swimming and doing their everyday normal activities (given the fact that they didn't know what had happened the previous night) and wondering to themselves why they couldn't be as free as the birds in the sky or fish in the sea. Each one, however, was very grateful to know this life has a purpose. None of us is put here by mere happenstance. We all have a "mission" to fulfill!

With sorrow in his heart and tears in his eyes, Philipiano said, "Well, I suppose the time has come that just sends my heart to someplace I don't want to visit, ever! The time has come to say goodbye. I want you all to know, however, I don't wish to leave, but I must. I guess I knew. I suppose I've always known. I just wasn't aware that it would come so quickly and so suddenly!"

Trying his best to remain aloof and not try to show his attraction to her until the last possible moment, Philipiano saw Linda tearing-up and thought to himself, *What must I do to make her happy again?*

Directing himself toward his newest, best friend, he said, "Don't worry, Linda, I'll be all right, I'll come back to see you and your betrothed."

She started to speak, and he immediately put a finger up to her mouth. "Shh! I don't know when, and I don't know how. But I imagine it will be in much the same way as when we first met." Thinking of how they met and the circumstances caused him to smile. It caused such a grin to come upon both of their faces that her parents became somewhat suspicious.

Trying his hardest to get his best friend's brother to board the boat, willingly, Giovanni tried to go beyond his own duties as first mate on this particular venture. He took Linda aside, and both of them spoke for hours, or so it seemed to Philipiano. He wasn't part of the conversation and therefore didn't want to interrupt. Something told him he shouldn't. *So,* he told himself, *She would rather talk to Giovanni, a man who up until about two months ago, she didn't know from Adam! Give me a break! I don't see how they can even be old friends!*

Philipiano could have sworn to have seen them kissing, but he couldn't be sure, so he decided to leave well enough alone. He said to himself, *I'm not too certain that I shouldn't get a brand-new traveling companion… NO! Now wake up! This entire fiasco is his fault! Why should I have to suffer? Arrgh! It's just not fair!* Isn't it funny how someone can lose sight of what's really important for the sake of the opposite sex? However, Philipiano had done just that!

Just at that precise moment, Giovanni let go of Linda, who had tears in her eyes. Philipiano thought maybe they had heard his thoughts, which he really didn't want to happen. Well, he may have wanted it a little bit, but at the same time, he didn't.

Giovanni sauntered over to the waiting boat with a smile on his face that stretched from ear to ear. He said, "Are you ready, then? Shall we go?" He began to feign impatience. He was like a kid in a candy store who wants everything he sees, but doesn't quite have the patience that his parents would like!

Looking down and to the right, amid tears of his own, because Philipiano didn't want to be viewed as a pansy, he said, "Help me understand something, won't you?"

"Sure. You know, I'll actually do anything for the kingdom, right? And since you, being royalty yourself, are basically the kingdom, I have been sworn to do anything you ask, within reason."

"Right." But Philipiano had other things in mind as he spoke. He somehow and in someway just had to ask, but he was afraid that he wouldn't like the answer. "What exactly did you and Linda speak about to each other?" All of a sudden, he realized that he should speak a little more properly, "ere, excuse me, I should know better, being the son of royalty, I should say 'about what, were you two speaking?'" He felt he understood his dad a little bit better, and he felt ashamed at the way he and Bartoloméo tried to keep Fitipaldi out of the loop.

"I'm sorry, but I'm not at liberty to say. I know it's tough on you right now, but you've got to be unusually strong on this one. Just trust me."

Has it ever occurred to him, thought Philipiano, *that he doesn't need to tell me to be strong, that maybe something just isn't right here? There are many, many who would have given their lives for this chance to search for me! What must I do to convince him of this fact?* After about a minute of this torture, he spoke, "I think you have," and grabbing Giovanni by the shirt, much like a villain would in a John Wayne movie, only he had underestimated Giovanni's strength, not to mention the fact that Giovanni was so much bigger and stronger than Philipiano could ever have imagined, along with the fact that he had forgotten, albeit temporarily, his oath to the king's son, to defend the kingdom at the cost of his very own life, "underestimated your strength. Either that, or I may have overestimated my own." Not really wanting to fight, in the first place, he continued, "but this is not the way I saw our friendship going. We both saw the Star. I think we need to reevaluate our actions and see where changes need to be made! I am sure the Son of God would not be pleased with either of us at this time."

They both let go of each other, and both began apologizing for their behavior. Suffice it to say: both of them felt sorry for having acted the way they did. "Man, Philipiano, you sure pack one awesome punch! I bet time will soon be able to tell us who, if either one, is the better man. Or, if neither you nor I is the strongest!"

"Yeah, I see your point," said Philipiano, gasping for breath. "We're pretty pathetic, aren't we?"

Giovanni being a fallen comrade made the following comment: "To think a girl, whose name shall remain unspoken, almost, and I do mean JUST ABOUT, came between us. I don't know what, exactly, came over me! Not to say that Linda is ugly, or anything. She's an extremely gorgeous girl. Do I make myself clear?"

"Yes, I think so." Still trying to recover from their fight, Philipiano was not in the best bargaining position he could be, or had been in his life. But he still had no idea what Giovanni and Linda were saying to each other. His "threats" didn't seem to work. At least, not as far as Giovanni was concerned. Johnny was too much man for Philipiano to handle. So, having thought about it some more, he tried a different approach. Besides, he had just about exhausted every other avenue known to him. He made an appeal to Giovanni's merciful side, but Johnny was having none of that! "Oh, come on. TELL me! You know you're dying to let me know."

However much Philipiano may have wanted to know, Giovanni was that dead set against telling him. Needless to say, it was a long, long, extremely boring boat ride home for our hero's brother. It seems silence permeated every fiber of their beings. Not a word was spoken by either one. There were, however, certain things that had to be said in order to maneuver safely to shore.

Chapter 15

As the ship neared the waiting harbor, a voice could be heard from the approaching ship. Only Bartoloméo, who had kept a vigilant eye on the water, knew. He also recognized the voice as Giovanni. "Watch out for the rocks. They can be deceptive! Careful, Philipiano. I'm too young to die!"

"I know how old you are! No need to tell *me*!" And Bartoloméo could swear he heard his brother say under his breath (and this really made his blood boil) "You're as old as my brother, and he's *ancient*! The two of you are more alike than either one of you realize!" But he wasn't sure if that was a slam, and if it was a slam, how should Bartoloméo react?

A former Bartoloméo would have been extremely irate, but ever since he was left alone, basically, to defend the kingdom, his appreciation, respect, adoration, love—not to mention his dependency—had grown stronger. He called out to them in a deep, baritone voice, "I thought you'd never make it back!"

Giovanni replied, "We almost didn't!"

"Really! And why is that?"

"Ask your brother! Besides, he's chosen not to talk to me, so you may as well be the one he tells."

Of course, Philipiano was just dying to divulge the past two, two and a half years to some one—he still didn't know how long it had been—yet it didn't matter to him. Time was just something on a clock. He was in love. He knew it. Anyone with half a brain should have suspected the same!

"Really?" Bartoloméo got this look in his eye like, "Wow, can I really be that important?"

"Yes!" Then looking off to Bartoloméo's right at some people who had just walked out onto the dock, Giovanni spotted his wife. She had heard a rumor that maybe a boat had made it to shore, and she was hoping that her husband was on board.

Her anxieties and fears were soon put to rest, as the sound of her name floated ever so gently on the wind. They ran toward each other and were caught up in the ecstasy of seeing each other after so long apart. "I never thought you'd make it back," she shrieked.

"I know! It was 'iffy' there for a while." He rehearsed to his wife the struggles he had getting Philipiano to actually want to come home with him. He borrowed a line from Bartoloméo, "It was all I could do to be standing here right now!"

As Giovanni and Nicole's reunion commenced, our story's hero was also being sought out by his own brother. And though a few years separated them, they became closer, according to Philipiano, than ever before. "Oh man, Bartoloméo, do I ever have a story to relate!"

"I thought you might, having been gone for so long. And do I have story for you! Did you see the sign? Well, I should hope so!" He provided for Philipiano a history of the events of the past two-and-a-half years. He knew how long his brother had been gone. There was no way Bartoloméo would allow his brother to forget that. He loved his brother, sure, but even the deepest love, and his father's threats of no use of his boat should he ever say anything to him about his mistakes, were of no use on him, at least not this time.

"There are a few things I would like to tell you, as well. I think I have fallen in love, finally! You'd like her! I think even dad would like her!" He always became so excited whenever he talked about her. With good reason, of course.

Bartoloméo almost snickered at the thought of Philipiano *ever* being in love. To him, it seemed almost as if the world was coming to an end. "I'm not ready for the world to be nonexistent! There is still so much I'd like to do." He then, jokingly, gazed upward toward heaven and added, "I'm too young to die!"

His brother looked at him sideways, and between laughter said, "You, young? Oh please!" And he started to make fun of his elder brother, but in a way which made Bartoloméo laugh himself, which wasn't easy to do. "Man, do you and I need to talk."

Bartoloméo's facial expression told Philipiano everything he needed, or wanted, to know. "Go on," he said, anticipating some earth shattering news. "But you can tell me as we are walking? You see, I've got to load the boat, before we can go. And I want to get going as soon as possible! I would've liked to have gone when I first saw the sign! Now that you're here, we can go!" He was so excited to leave, he didn't even think of asking his brother if he wanted to go along. However, he soon realized he needed to ask before they left. "Hey, how would you like to go on another adventure?"

"I can't. I think someone in this family had better stay, and since you are so bent on going, I'll stay and look after dad." He said that behind a smile. "Besides, I think it would be best if you were to go. It's not like you don't already know about a thousand languages! I'm sure you don't want me tagging along. It's not like I could be of much help if your were to get mixed up with the 'sea gods,' who, I hear, are pretty treacherous." Bartoloméo's smile reminded Philipiano of Carlos. That's how much he missed Linda and the island life. He found he was even amazed at how much he was missing Linda's dad, too. In fact, there was nothing that didn't remind him of the happiest time of his life, so far.

After speaking to each other a little more, Bartoloméo finally said, "Tell me about Linda! I mean, I know you already have, somewhat." He always tried to help others express themselves—their hopes, dreams, desires. "Leave nothing out!" He wanted details.

"I don't know where to begin."

Bartoloméo just looked at his brother without guile and without hypocrisy, and said, "The beginning is usually the best place."

Having anticipated this moment for quite some time, Philipiano took a deep breath and began: "On the day I left, I felt as though no one loved me. Come to find out, however, I was wrong. Go ahead, tease me. I'm sure that you've wanted to do so ever since I returned. But I'm telling you, you would have wanted to stay as well. Although, I'm pretty sure *you* wouldn't have gotten as far with her as I did. Which, while it may have been too much for you to handle, wasn't quite enough for me!" Just another attempt to make himself much better than his brother. Although Bartoloméo really had no idea what his brother was trying to do.

Philipiano continued, "Her smile is, by far, the best smile I've ever seen in my life. Her eyes are like the stars in the heavens. And she has a body that just won't quit!" He shouted that last bit about her body to exaggerate his point. Of course, many men would describe the woman with whom they are in love in much the same way. "I'm not sure why we are even talking about this, because she is betrothed." Tears began to form in his young but proud eyes. He could have been mistaken for the Iguazu Falls had they not lived within a few days' travel. However, recovering himself he added, "Law and the fact that her own father has already promised her to someone else will keep us apart."

Bartoloméo could see that his brother was really in love this time. What about the other times? What about Ginny? He'd been totally smitten by her, had he not? Even in some weird and twisted way, Philipiano had felt—although he was way off base with this one—that Broomhelda was in love with him. Before he knew it, Philipiano was singing to himself, "Anytime you want me…anytime you need me… I'm standing here, with my arms a mile wide."

Bartoloméo could stand it no longer. "If you are just going to sing, and not help, I have a suggestion. I have it on good authority that mom is not busy. Why don't you go sing your troubles to her? Besides, we have a lot of work to do, if I'm going to present father's gold to the Son of God."

"Hey, you're so right! How can I help?"

"Really? You actually want to help? If that's true, you could start by handing me some of father's gold. Do you know where he keeps it?"

Bartoloméo was just about to say something else, but Philipiano beat him to it, "I know where it is, no need to be so condescending!" He had had some problems as a boy coveting his dad's gold. He had gotten himself into serious trouble by gambling, which was something he knew to be wrong. But because he felt luck was on his side, he'd tried it. Needless to say, he lost. Boy, had he ever gotten a whipping that night. He never returned to gambling. Bartoloméo had played a bigger role in that than Philipiano realized. Bartoloméo became the enforcer. Whenever Philipiano had as much as stepped out of the house, he'd been followed for some time by his parole officer of a brother.

Philipiano continued to watch, with some fascination, as Bartoloméo loaded the boat. He found himself becoming quite jealous, although he didn't know exactly why. He couldn't help but think, *If I had only NOT gone on that stupid adventure… but then again, I wouldn't have had the best two-and-a-half years OF MY LIFE! So I'm glad I went.*

Bartoloméo was glad as well that Philipiano had gone on his own little adventure. Because, had Philipiano stayed, he probably would have been tagging along, and Bartoloméo wouldn't have been able to "bash" his brother like he secretly wanted. "Giovanni, be sure to grab a couple of fishing rods. I don't want to starve to death!"

Giovanni looked up at him from his post, and with a wry smile responded, "Already done!"

"Good! Somehow I knew I could count on you!" Bartoloméo looked around to find his younger brother and added in a very loud voice, "unlike some people I know!"

Chapter 16

N ear modern-day Panama City is a place where there used to be a great river connecting the "sea East," with the "sea West." This existed before the death of Christ. It was a mighty river, which ran deep and slow. So slow, in fact, that it was often mistaken for the ocean itself. In fact, great fishes swam there. Fitipaldi himself was known for his fishing prowess. He could often be seen there teaching Bartoloméo basic survival skills or sailing techniques.

Bartoloméo and Giovanni put the boat in the water and set sail. Millions of others have done so, without being aware of who, exactly, sailed these waters before. Only, they sailed west, as opposed to Philipiano, who had sailed east.

Had he gone with them, Philipiano surely would have caused them to lose another day's travel. Because he, most likely, would have wanted to stop at Sicily. They were already behind, and neither Bartoloméo nor Giovanni wanted to get behind any more than was necessary. They both knew it was necessary to be waylaid at various times, due to their need to eat if they wanted to survive.

Both were extremely glad 'King Phil' decided not to tag along, even though, just before they left, Philipiano had given them a present from Fitipaldi—a compass. It was so they wouldn't lose their way home. It had made Bartoloméo cry, which was something that Philipiano didn't want to see—ever!

As they left the shore behind, Bartoloméo said, "This compass reminds me of happier times. Do you remember when we were younger and we each made little toy boats, out of these compasses?"

Giovanni looked at him with a confused look on his face, as if he were trying to remember but couldn't. In reality, however, he didn't want to remember. His childhood was not something he cared to revisit that often. He didn't know why; he just didn't like the man he used to be. However, there were some happy times he had spent with Bartoloméo that made him smile. "Same here! Hey, do you know what else? It reminds me of a dream I had once of Philipiano. Did I ever tell you about it?"

"No, I don't believe I've ever had the privilege. You never allowed me to see that side of you." And smiling at his friend he added, "I didn't know you played for *that* team." He was trying to make Giovanni feel embarrassed.

Giovanni tried to play along. So, instead of being offended, he began acting the part of a "fairy" young fellow by tilting his wrist forward and speaking with a certain "tilt" in his voice: a je no sè qua. Bartoloméo didn't know what it meant either, but he sure didn't want to find out. "You didn't know? What are we going to do with you?"

"I don't know," Bartoloméo said, "but can I get back to what I was saying, please? Thank you. As I was saying, it sure is a good thing Philipiano didn't come with us. It's a good thing for two reasons. A) we don't have to put up with his womanizing and, 2) we won't need to change him, especially if we run into any sea monsters!"

That seemed to get the desired response out of Giovanni. They both reared their heads back and laughed, causing them to shed tears. But all jokes aside, Bartoloméo actually respected and loved his brother dearly. Philipiano, too, loved and respected his brother enormously. It was almost necessary, because both knew of the other's ability to sail—that was never a problem. But it was the way Philipiano complained about *everything* that drove our protagonist up a wall.

"Anyway, as I was saying before we started talking about this now hopefully ancient memory of a brother of mine—and please don't take this the wrong way, because I don't wish him any ill will or anything of the sort. I just get so sick and tired of his antics. He drives me crazy!"

Of course, Giovanni had agreed. It was bad enough to be sailing on these waters, which were more deadly and frightful than anything he had ever seen. There was talk back home about great sea monsters, but to actually be sailing with someone you'd prefer not, especially an ex-best friend, was not particularly something he even wanted to attempt. Besides, he felt that perhaps Bartoloméo had already done enough for him. He loved Bartoloméo, sure, but he was still scared. Although, he had no reason to be because Bartoloméo would defend him at the cost of his very own life.

Giovanni knew this to be true because of the time when they were younger and Bartoloméo had saved him from almost certain death on the Iguazu Falls. He may have known this to be true, but the level of friendship they had—of which there could be no equal, anywhere—was dangerous. Because even the best of friends still have the possibility of an argument.

That argument could cost them the best friendship they had possibly ever known.

There was no way Giovanni would ever do anything to come between Bartoloméo and his brother, for he had witnessed firsthand their love for one another. He didn't want to get mixed up in or cause a family squabble. He could have become the third wheel on their family two-man bicycle, but let's just say he changed his mind.

"Anyway, as I was saying. Before the *man* who shall not be named…" he said "man" so as to indicate his brother, but he could hold back his emotions no longer. "I'm about to break my own cardinal rule and mention his name… Philipiano." He started to break down in a flood of emotions. However, he didn't want to appear weak in front of his friend, so he became the man he knew he was and sternly commanded, "Right rudder full!" He had no idea what that meant, but he had heard his dad say it numerous times when he was being taught how to sail, and he felt it gave his dad more authority. He thought he'd do the same.

Giovanni followed Bartoloméo's orders to the letter. After all, Bartoloméo was experienced and knew how to sail. Of that there could be no question. He just seemed to imitate his dad when giving orders. Besides, how else could he let the "natural man" appear?

"Careful, Bartoloméo, you're beginning to get a big head," cried Giovanni. He didn't want to experience any more difficulties or hardships in his life. "I don't think we need to pull down the wrath of a just God upon us. I fear you're about to do just that!"

Thoughts of his great uncle began to take over his mind. Was there nothing he could do, either, to escape "the ghost of Teancum"? Apparently God had a great work in store for him, as well. "I know what I'm doing, my friend. I know what I'm doing. Only, I'm not quite sure as to where we are going!" He felt like he should have ordered his friend to take over, but then because of his fear of the unknown, he felt he shouldn't say a word.

"I'll tell you where we are going, but first tell me why you are being so…" Giovanni started snapping his fingers, and without even knowing it he was imitating Fitipaldi. Yet at the same time, he was also imitating one of Bartoloméo's great uncles. He kept snapping, as if searching for the right words. Finally, he added, "…boastful, high minded, and proud? I'm afraid you're getting out of control! We don't need any of that while we're on the ocean. We might drown, do you hear me!? Now I'm trying to do that which we should be doing, which is giving glory to the Son of God! Something for which, I believe, *you* volunteered me! Now, don't get me wrong, I actually DO want to go! It's just that I don't want to lose my life in the process!"

Bartoloméo, behind loving eyes, said, "I don't think you're going to lose your life. But rather, you'll find it!"

"What do you mean?" said Giovanni. "I don't know how you figure I'll find it when I already know who I am. I'm not so sure I follow you."

Still looking at him somewhat tenderly, because Bartoloméo wanted to be the teacher in this case, he added, "It's quite simple, really." He started quoting Isaiah, a man who he admired almost as much as his own father. However, he knew and trusted the latter more. He felt as though he were a Prophet himself, and he probably was. Although, there was no way to put his theories, teachings, and prophecies to the test. In fact, the only thing he had going for him was the fact that he believed another man's words. But could that be enough? Apparently so, since the testimony of Jesus Christ is the spirit of prophecy. "Plus the fact that you're going with me to witness His birth. That should be enough, shouldn't it?" He then grabbed his friend around the shoulders and began to shake, although, he did it in the most delightful way imaginable. They were, after all, best friends. Then, each thought, *would a prophet of God act this way?* For they were having a wrestling match, and having the time of their lives.

Before they knew it, they were approaching what is now known as Hawaii. Upon arriving, they both saw an old friend who was also delighted to see them.

CHAPTER 17

As they reached the shore, they were greeted by some old friends—because the Hawaiians had to have come from somewhere; why not from the same place as the ancient inhabitants of Bartoloméo's land? In fact, they were the same who had sailed with Hagar when he left the "old land." The only problem was that Hagar was far too ambitious for his own good. He wanted power and authority. He wanted it so badly, he didn't really care about those who had helped him cross the ocean to get to his new home. As a matter of fact, he had become a self-proclaimed king. Things were looking extremely good for him, at first, just as they had for the Nephites. But once again, that green-eyed monster made himself known, causing all peace to be lost. No one from the old world knew about these wars. They simply had lost all communication. A history of the Hawaiians will not be given, as more and more people will find it out in due time. Suffice it to say, they are—as we all are—descended from the same gene code.

As descendents from literally the same gene pool, they were prone to the same kinds of pride, riches, and temptations as all of us, but there is no need to allow the devil to succeed. This is part of a history we'd rather not know.

A man named Samuel and his son greeted our heroes in an amiable manner, which helped make the Hawaiian culture famous. "What brings you to this island and so far from home?"

Giovanni, who was near the front of the boat, was the first to speak , "We're going to Jerusalem to witness the birth of the Savior of the world. We wanted to know if you would like to come along with us. Bartoloméo's father has generously shared some of his gold. In fact, this boat is loaded to the brim. We were wondering if you would like to contribute as well?" He was extremely shy as he asked the question, almost as if he were embarrassed because he felt as though what they had was not enough. "Who can give enough to the Son of God? All He asks of us is the heart! Yet, how many of us are not even willing to give Him *that*? If you had the blessings He *wants* to give you, you'd be wealthier than anything you could imagine. However, He does require a certain sacrifice on our part. He won't just hand out His blessings, willy-nilly. If you are true and faithful to His commandments, you are on your way!" Once again, if you don't know what you should be doing, you are strongly advised to find the missionaries and ask them. They won't tell you you're going to hell, or anything (which does exist, by the way) but you won't be able to reach your full potential either. Bartoloméo and Giovanni knew this to be hell, in its own right. If we were to not reach our full potential, they would be very disappointed, not to mention the Savior himself! All of the characters in this story knew that we are not placed here by mere happenstance, but to fulfill a certain purpose.

"I don't think I can go with you," Samuel responded, but my son Samuel would be able to go in my place." He looked somewhat sorrowful saying this, because he also wanted to go.

Once again, Giovanni spoke, "Arrgh, we really wanted you to come!"

"I'm sure, but it's just not possible." As much as he wanted to, he couldn't: the Hawaiians had grown tired of Hagar's role as monarch of the island, and Samuel had already promised them he would help fight for their freedom. "But if you were to let my son Samuel go, it would be the same as if I myself were to go, would it not?"

Bartoloméo could hold his silence no longer. He showed his emotions, finally, by letting a huge yelp of excitement, which could be heard in his hometown. "I didn't know you would contribute as well! Yet, even I had some doubts of whether anyone else would contribute to our quest." Looking at Giovanni with even more respect he added, "Way to go, my friend!" He showed his approval by giving the thumbs-up sign. It's supposed that, even back then, they knew the universal sign of approval.

Feeling embarrassed, somewhat, Giovanni said, "Oh, you're too kind!" He jokingly started acting again the part of a fairy young fellow.

Once he had boarded the boat, Samuel turned to Bartoloméo: "I'm so excited to be going with you guys! I can't wait to see the Son of the Most High! Shouldn't I also find something to take to Him? After all, this is a once-in-a-lifetime opportunity. We're privileged beyond anything anyone else can even imagine!" He started to shed tears of gratitude. He looked around and discovered he wasn't alone in his feelings. "Did you see the sign as well? It was the most beautiful thing anyone, anywhere could ever have witnessed! And most of the world probably won't care, one way or the other."

"I know. It's all rather sad, isn't it?" groaned Bartoloméo. "To think they all have the same chance as we, to worship the Son of God, and they're not taking advantage. It breaks the heart. And to think we almost didn't come, all because of my younger brother and his following his no-good, lousy, broken, and sad heart. Well, you've met her, Giovanni, what's she like?"

To say Giovanni became embarrassed by the question would be an understatement. He wanted to play down Linda's beauty but found no reason to lie: "She's a wonder to behold!" He became extremely passive; probably more so than ever. Until finally he shot this look at his friend, like a light bulb had just ignited itself in his head. "Hey Bartoloméo, I may have done something completely stupid." And shyly, he related to his best friend the events that had taken place right before their departure and what he had said to Linda. He'd explained that Philipiano would probably come looking for her and how she should wait to get married until she, at least, gave him a chance. That would explain why it looked, to Philipiano, as though they were kissing. Linda had just been so happy. Giovanni, of course, "didn't want to be rude." So, he more than gladly accepted her embrace, which he justified to himself.

This conversation made Bartoloméo smile, knowing he would have something to hold over his brother's head. Only, he didn't count on Giovanni's following advice: "Don't let your brother, who shall remain nameless, ever know about this conversation. As far as he's concerned, it never took place. Got it? Good!"

Samuel Sr., who was loading some supplies onto their boat, stopped what he was doing and became a busybody, "Who shall remain nameless?"

Bartoloméo stepped forward, and with a very sorrowful look on his face said, "It's not really important."

"Why's that?" Inquired Samuel Jr., who had a hard time understanding why anyone in their right mind would allow such a chance as this to pass.

Giovanni said, "It's not really something Bartoloméo wishes to discuss at the moment. Perhaps as time passes, he will open his heart to us, but for now, I think we should respect his wishes and just let it die."

Samuel couldn't understand the reason why Bartoloméo became so sad whenever anyone so much as mentioned his brother's name. Yet they were so friendly toward each other. Was it just a ruse? A game? What was it about these two that was so hard to figure? What was it that they wanted to keep so secret? He made a personal vow to bring down Giovanni's best friend's barriers while on this trip. "Why is it you don't like to talk about your brother? There must be a reason! Help me understand, won't you?"

Once again, Giovanni stepped forward, "It's not really that important. We'll try to tell you on this trip. But for now, just let it die. Besides, we'll need your strength to help man the boat."

"Okay, I'll be quiet, for now. But be expecting a lot of questions!" he said behind a smile.

They continued to sail west, and finally Samuel said, "Do you guys mind if we take a different route? I think Prince Yasser, from the island where they do that funky kind of dance, would like to go as well." He explained a bit about karate and how it works. "They say it's self-defense, but to me it looks more like a dance. Go figure!"

Giovanni was standing next to him. "I think I know how it goes." And he began lifting his left leg, while keeping the right one firmly planted, "It's like this. When the attacker gets brave enough to come forward, because he doesn't know you know what you're doing, you let him have it with the right foot." He's tried his best to demonstrate, and fell.

Bartoloméo had noticed by this time that there was no further need to steer the boat, and he decided to join in on the conversation. He was, of course, included already. "I thought I'd join in this little discussion. After all, the wind is freshening. It appears to be smooth sailing from here on out! Anyone care not to stop by Yasser's Island? Because if you'd rather not stop, I can arrange it. But if you're like me and want to go, I can arrange that, too!" He smiled.

CHAPTER 18

B artolomeo heard a chorus of what seemed to him to be approval, in fact, he just about went deaf. As they neared the island of Japan, Giovanni noticed that his stomach was growling. Not one of them had a chance to eat anything, due to the fact that prince Samuel had become rather ill because he had a piece of what he trusted to be "edible" fish. The others had all eaten it, too. Besides, he had grown-up eating that particular fish, so he figured it was edible. He was wrong—dead wrong! Luckily for the others, he wasn't contagious—at least not overtly contagious. However, they still did their best to avoid him.

King Yasser's castle was so foreboding it provoked fear. He really was an ostentatious man who liked having power. With its king-size beds and gigantic bedrooms to match, one could easily say he loved his wealth. He flaunted it, as did Hagar. You might say he was without shame. There were prisons for those who ever opposed him. Thankfully for the citizens, these were empty. Because of his type of rule, no one dared oppose him. He had servants who did their best to please him. They really tried to honor the king, but more out of fear than love! Whereas, the Nephites felt they should obey their kings' commands out of respect and love. The Nephites, also knew their king would only be in power for as long as God wanted.

Giovanni was reminded of what Philipiano had told him about Sicily, for the people of the island nation of Japan were also slaves to their emperor. Then again, he knew deep down in his heart that it needn't be so; all men are created equal.

After their arrival to the island nation of Japan, which they had approached with some trepidation for fear of the unknown, they were greeted by the king himself: Yasser, whose son just happened to be named, Yasser, as well. Immediately Giovanni thought, *Why can't anyone be original? Don't these people know that we are not clones, but people? We all have our idiosyncrasies that make us each unique? Sometimes, I'm astounded at how unoriginal people can be. What would they do if they were to give birth to just girls, name them all Yassiera? I suppose SHE would pass the name Yasser to her children!*

81

Samuel had just about broken his leg as he tried getting out of the boat. Apparently, he was so excited to see his Japanese friend, he didn't take into account the dangers of exiting a boat that was still in motion! However, upon seeing his friend practically "called home to that God who had given him life," Prince Yasser also left his post prematurely, causing King Yasser to lose what little mind he had. It's bad enough to see a friend of your son almost lose his life by trying to exit a still moving boat, but to see your son pretty much abandon duty to the kingdom in order to see someone you don't even know all that well… "Howdy, my old friend. What brings you out this far?" Prince Yasser said.

In his broken down Japanese, Samuel said, "We are on our way to Jerusalem to witness the birth of our Savior. Would you care to go along with us? We are all taking gifts."

Based on what he saw, Prince Yasser was floored. He didn't know what to say, but the glittering gold made him covet that which he couldn't have. He behaved as an alcoholic who tries to get one last drink but the bar has already closed for the night. Finally he said, "Really! I am afraid you have no myrrh to give Him."

Both Giovanni and Bartoloméo had puzzled looks on their faces. They didn't really understand. They tried, oh how they tried, to get the meaning of the gift, but they'd never heard of it. "What does it do exactly?"

"I like to think of it as a balm."

"A bomb? What, do you want to kill us all?" Then they both began to run around as if they were chickens with their heads cut off, screaming those words.

"No! It's not a bomb, but a BALM! More for cuts and scrapes and little boo-boos you may get from time to time."

Samuel, who had just about broken his leg as he left the security of a plush boat to see someone he hadn't seen in years, lifted his leg and asked, "Like this?"

With an overwhelming sense of pride, Prince Yasser replied, "Exactly!" Smiling from ear to ear, he looked at Samuel's leg and joked, "Does someone need his mommy? Oh, you poor baby!" He continued to make jabs at his friend to win the approval of his other traveling companions, about whom he had already been informed by Samuel. He was really a shy guy who had absolutely no friends, which explains why he was so good at karate. Instead of hanging out with friends, he devoted his life to the practice of self-defense. He was not a very big person. In fact, he was deceitfully small but exceptionally strong and fast. He was able to get away with just about anything, so it's no wonder that opposing him (if you were to dare) would be equivalent to facing more pain than you could possibly imagine! He was like Bartoloméo in many respects, only not quite as large. He had the same build as Giovanni with only a few minor differences. You could say, because of their similarities, that they were twins who were separated at birth.

All of a sudden, King Yasser, who had been standing nearby, spoke: "Have you eaten since you left Prince Samuel's?" Those are the words a worried father, even if he wasn't all that original, would say. When everyone said they hadn't, the king didn't dare let them travel on empty stomachs, so he invited them to be his guests for dinner, which everyone more than gladly accepted. "Jerusalem is only about a one-day sail. Either that or two days. Only, you have to have a good feeling about your trip. You can't just sail haphazardly, but you must have a plan, and nowhere else can you sail. The waters can be pretty dangerous. It might help if you know what you're doing."

Each one of them began to snicker one to the other, because they were all pretty good sailors. Even the prince—Yasser's son—knew how to sail. Yet for some reason this king couldn't trust anyone. It isn't known why, exactly. It may have been because when he was younger he too was wreckless and carefree. He could have cared less about the world around him. He and his son were very much alike in that neither one was very responsible. Finally the king concluded, "I suppose that since you're going to see this world's creator, you can go with my blessing."

All of them graciously prostrated themselves, "Thank you!"

Both Giovanni and Bartoloméo became somewhat emotional at hearing the prince could go. Both certainly hoped he could, for they knew deep in their hearts that it was the right thing to do. In fact, there wasn't a single person in their party who didn't know it was the right thing to do. Even though there was a language barrier (they basically had to speak through Samuel, who had to speak through prince Yasser: it was touch and go for a while) they were able to communicate. After having been fed the most delectable meal they had eaten in a while (no thanks to Samuel, and his weak stomach) they once again committed themselves to that God who gave them life.

CHAPTER 19

As they commenced their journey, Giovanni noticed a dark cloud in front of them from his post atop the ship. He began to think of his wife, Nicole, which he tended to do a bit too often, and how much the cloud reminded him of her. But then again, there wasn't much of anything that didn't remind him of her. He was in a daze—the kind from which you don't wish to be awoken. He felt the gentle lapping of the ocean breeze and how it gently caressed his cheeks, just as she would do. He was a hopeless romantic. Whenever he thought of her he was a daydreaming fool who didn't know up from down, right from left, or nighttime from daytime. But thankfully he came out of his self-induced coma just in time to warn the others of the impending doom. However, they were on a mission to give glory to the Son of God! So, with that thought in mind, he felt there was no way they could possibly be in any sort of danger! What he didn't realize was that maybe God is no respecter of persons. It doesn't matter—or seem to matter—what the mission is. Trials will come into the lives of the best of us. God wants to see just how faithful we will be. Perhaps that is why we have trials in our lives even when we think we are doing our best.

As the storm came closer and the waves grew larger, Bartoloméo, in his unmistakable, huge, powerful, baritone voice asked, "What's going on? Why is this pool of water forming around my feet? Does my best friend need to be relieved of his duties? Does my best friend need his mommy?"

"No!" Clearly, Giovanni was frustrated. "I have everything under control! I've got it." Then the self-doubts began: "At least I think I've got it. It's all under control, isn't it?" He was starting to feel the pressure of being responsible for more than just his own life. He was a very accomplished sailor, in his own right, but never before had he been in this position. It raised him up to what he had never thought possible. He actually placed the feeling of being needed—finally—with the feeling of euphoria.

This caused Bartoloméo to smile at the thought of being responsible for teaching Giovanni how to sail. He would have liked to take responsibility for his best friend's abilities, but there was no way Fitipaldi would relinquish that honor, not even to his own flesh and blood! For Fitipaldi had been the one to teach Bartoloméo. Bartoloméo called back up to his friend: "Oh, it is under control, is it?" He had a hard time believing even his best friend. "Let's see how much you have it all under control! I hope you're not lying to me!"

Giovanni didn't take offense at his remarks, because even he knew that he wasn't the best sailor to ever be entrusted with so many lives. He knew, or thought he knew, as much as Bartoloméo. But with the impending storm on the horizon: he knew he couldn't make it through without help from someone who knew just a little more than he did. "Hey, Bartoloméo!" He was really starting to worry now. "I don't see any way around this storm. I hate to say it, but I'm afraid that we'll all lose our lives trying to make it through!"

Heroically, Bartoloméo grabbed the stern, trying not to show up his best friend, "I don't see what the problem is! You're doing a fine job! So what if the waves are trying to make us go topside. They won't take me down without a fight!"

Samuel and Yasser, who had been sleeping the entire time, arose from their small but restful beds. "What's the problem?" they asked, while rubbing their eyes, stretching, and yawning "Here we were in the most beautiful and sweet dreams you could possibly imagine only to be awoken in a violent and disturbing manner! Do you need any help?"

Doing his best to be brave and not show any emotion whatsoever to his friends, Giovanni said, "What's the problem? I thought I said I have everything under control!"

At that precise moment, Yasser just happened to look at the horizon, and he saw the same thing that Giovanni and Bartoloméo had seen: an ominous cloud with no way around it. "What are we going to do? I'm too young to die!"

A very distraught but strong Giovanni fixed his gaze—which had been completely focused on the horizon, but now was a little worried—on Yasser and became somewhat defensive. "If you have any ideas on how to make this a more enjoyable experience for everyone," he let go of the helm in exasperation and threw his hands in the air, "be my guest!" This entire conversation took place through Samuel. And as anyone who has ever had to speak through an interpreter can attest: it's absolutely no fun! It may seem romantic, but in the end it is the worst experience you could possibly want!

To say Yasser was apologetic would be an understatement, "Would it be best if the rest of us were just to allow you, and you alone, to sail this boat? Is that what you're saying?"

"Yes, I suppose it is." From that moment on, they became better friends. "But you best latch onto something secure!"

He was right! Danger lurked ahead! They were headed for certain destruction. It was the largest and most powerful, and threatening typhoon any of them had ever seen. The waves of the ocean were as high as any sea monster they could have possibly imagined. Each was extremely terrified at the thought of dying at such a young age. Samuel and Yasser both grabbed hold of Bartoloméo for dear life! Giovanni would have as well, but he was too busy trying to guide the boat through the impending doom! Trying to keep the others out of harm's way was rather exhausting work. They cried to their God, each one of them praying in unison, "Please, mighty Father, save us!"

Almost instantly, the clouds began to disperse, the winds and waves subsided, and the sun appeared. Then from somewhere they could hear a voice. It wasn't a harsh voice, nor was it a loud voice. It was more than that, only it did pierce them to the very center: "They who fear me, and delight in worshiping me: their sins are forgiven them. They shall have eternal life, and shall sit down with me in the kingdom which I have prepared for them in the mansions of my Father. Yea, verily I say unto you, if this be the desire of your hearts, and you worship me, by keeping all of my commandments and doing that which I have sent you to do: verily, verily I say unto you, ye shall have eternal life!"

This was a promise which was made to a few, but it can be realized by all! And just think about it: all we have to do is worship the Son, our Savior, with all our might, mind, and strength! If we truly love Him like we should, we would feel an inclination to worship more than just once a year, and we would try harder to keep ourselves unspotted.

CHAPTER 20

They continued to sail in a northwestern direction. Not one of them dared speak; that is how much they respected the voice they had heard.

Giovanni noticed that they had all become as zombies,—walking around aimlessly, until he decided to break the tension. "Wow! That's all my mind will allow me to say: wow!"

"It was quite miraculous, wasn't it?" said a rather confused but elated Bartoloméo, who was still the self-proclaimed leader of the group. At this point, no one dared question his authority.

Samuel, who had decided to go in search of more fish to eat, said, "I have something to say, as well. It was the most miraculous thing I've ever had the privilege of witnessing." He looked around at everyone, saw that he had everyone's attention and continued, "I live in this part of the world that doesn't give me an ounce of hope. And I'm afraid that no one will believe a single word of what just happened. How do you suggest I explain it?"

Yasser, who was next to Samuel, also decided to be heard: "Excuse, please! I am very sorry, but I'm afraid I don't understand anything that's being said."

Bartoloméo, who was standing nearby and thought this would be a good time to teach (he thought this on a consistent basis, which was okay by him) said, "Did you understand the voice we just heard? It was the voice of God!" He started to become very jubilant, praising God. "Do you guys, in your nation, believe in God, too?" He expected him to say they didn't. He had this huge presentation prepared, in hopes of being able to emerge from this trip as a great missionary, like his personal heroes Ammon, Aaron, Omner, and Himni.

He had never expected to hear, "Yes."

"You do, do you? And how exactly, do you believe?" Only in the fire of affliction can one truly appreciate Bartoloméo's desire to make sure the world is converted. But he still trusts the reader won't read too much into what he calls the best experience one could possibly ever wish to have. And he felt he would be unwise if he didn't share what he knew to be true!

Once again, Yasser nodded his head, only this time he did it more out of frustration, like you might do to someone who only wants you to see his point of view but just doesn't seem to understand that you already agree with him because he's too proud to admit it and for some reason feels the necessity of proving he's right. It's very frustrating. You want to agree with everything that is being said—and you do—but you can't get a word in edgewise. Finally Yasser said, "But, what would you say, if I were to tell you, I agree?" Yasser couldn't have been more humble.

Samuel decided Yasser had had enough, "Why don't you leave the poor guy alone. He hasn't done anything. The one to whom you should be asking those questions is standing in front of you now." The one thing that simply amazed Bartoloméo was the fact that no one raised his voice. It was just a quiet conversation.

"So, I see," replied Bartoloméo. He went from being the group leader to a just plain, ordinary member. He was better off that way, anyway. Probably because he didn't have to deal any longer with the pressure of being in charge. It felt strange to him to no longer be the decision maker. While it was nice to have three other lives counting on him, he was tired of trying to get the others, "to be in constant agreement on all decisions." He apologized to Yasser and to the rest of the group. He didn't mean to act so cocky. "It's just in my nature," he explained.

Of course they all agreed to take part in being a leader from time to time. For each one brought different talents and abilities with himself. Even though Bartoloméo wanted Giovanni to go, and Giovanni wanted Samuel to go, and Samuel wanted Yasser to tag along: there are few people who could agree in a situation such as this. But they decided, and the keyword is *they*, that all decisions would be by common consent.

They continued to sail, only now they were headed more in a western direction. They passed the country known as Yemen, by the southern tip of Saudi Arabia. It reminded Giovanni of the Iberian Peninsula. "This all looks far too familiar," he said. Of course, no one else had the most remote idea what he was saying.

Bartoloméo's curiosity was stronger than their friendship, "Whatever do you mean?"

"I mean, if you ever had to go past the Iberian Peninsula, you'd know what I mean. Only the best and most experienced sailors can pass by there." He started to become cocky. Bartoloméo began to see himself in Giovanni, and he began to be somewhat frightened. "Because of your brother, I was forced to sail those waters." And suddenly like a flash of lightning that strikes you from out of the blue, he remembered that he shouldn't speak of his best friend's brother like he was a major part of the group. "Sorry, forgive me?"

"This time. But if it ever happens again…" Bartoloméo then punched his right fist into his awaiting left palm. The entire time he was smiling from ear to ear so Giovanni would know that they were still friends.

"Okay, it won't. But see to it you don't ever threaten me again!" Giovanni was also committed to their friendship, so he decided to return the smile.

Sailing north now, they passed by what today is known as the Suez Canal, where they could catch a faint glimpse of the pyramids, which made them all "ooh" and "aah" like never before. With the exception of maybe Bartoloméo, who was pretty hard to impress—ever. He was still very much taken aback by the ingenuity. "I just can't get over their creativity, their workmanship."

Before they knew it, they were back in the Mediterranean Sea and decided to turn their faces to the east, toward Jerusalem, because the star was still in the heavens, even though it was day, and all of the stars had pretty much died down for the day. The New Star, however, was still very much visible. They were certainly glad of that, because without the star they would have lost their way many times over.

As it turns out, it was all divine guidance. The Star was still obvious to everyone. And still it hung right over the place where Jesus lay.

CHAPTER 21

They pulled up to the harbor, after hearing Giovanni's immortal words, "Land ho!" After a few more minutes, and showing his cabin fever and eagerness to leave the boat, Giovanni asked, "Where do you suppose He has been born?"

Samuel was standing right behind him. "I don't know. Let's start by asking a few of the local crowd if they know where He is." Of course, they had all agreed because each one of them knew of their decision. This they had to do, because the star was pretty much over the entire town, now giving no further guidance.

Bartoloméo suggested they look for a local king, "Because he should know the goings-on in his kingdom." He saw a group of men huddled around a fire to keep themselves warm. "Perhaps we should ask them."

Yasser fearlessly approached the group and asked, "Are you gentlemen aware of where you have the potential to go, after this life?"

To say that the others were shocked at this new discovery that Yasser could speak Aramaic—and fluently—would be an understatement. It was just enough to make them all want to question him independent of each other. But the men to whom he had been speaking just looked at him sideways—kind of like they shouldn't be talking to him, as if they were superior to him because he wasn't a Jew. "All right, do you not wish to speak to me because I'm not a Jew!?"

He got into a self-defense stance—kind of a Ralph Maccio look from the Karate Kid series mixed in with a Crouching Tiger Hidden Dragon pose—and let them have it. He was fierce. They were scared of this "infidel." They had never seen his equal before and were not about to tempt fate.

One man broke out in tears and said, "My name is Beneton. I am the man with whom you want to speak. I saw the star for which you are looking." There was a pause. "It rested right over my stable. It was beautiful!"

This statement was met by a chorus of agreement, and Bartoloméo said, "We saw the same star in our homelands, too!"

"Oh you did, did you?" Beneton replied rather smugly, almost as if to say, "We are better than you, by far." However, this did not deter our heroes in any way. Nor did it stop Beneton, even though Bartoloméo and his group wanted him to be quiet. "Anyway, as I was telling you, I tried to allow them to stay, but there was just no room in the Inn." He started to sound whiny and desperate, and rubbing his hands together, to give himself more of a miserly look, said, "I sure do love tax season. It's very good for business!"

Bartoloméo had decided long, long ago that if things weren't going exactly how he wanted, he would have to resort to violence. However, he didn't have a violent bone in his body, so he would let Yasser fight this time. Beneton took one look at Yasser and knew he would need some reinforcements. Bartoloméo turned toward Giovanni: "I knew there was a reason I liked this guy."

"I thought maybe you'd say that," Giovanni whispered back, not wanting to offend, because he personally didn't want to become Yasser's enemy. Not that *anyone* in the group would ever desire to be the enemy of anyone else.

"Did you, now?" replied an astonished Bartoloméo.

"You bet. I had my doubts about him, but now I see no reason why he should have been left behind. His 'funky' dance will prove to be of more worth than we give him credit. Not to mention how fearless he is." And leaning forward to make his point a little more forceful he added, "He's definitely someone you want on your side."

Stepping forward himself, Bartoloméo gently placed one of his hands on Yasser's back, trying to get his attention. "I don't believe the Savior of the world would have you act like this."

Yasser turned himself around and took one good, long, hard look at Bartoloméo, who suddenly discovered that he didn't want to get involved in this after all. "Which is easier," Yasser snarled, "my way of intimidation and actually getting results, or your way, which I might add, almost got us killed at sea."

Thinking he had "made a friend," and reeking of alcohol, Beneton finally began to tell his tale. "I've never been so ashamed in all my life." He started to blubber. "No one will recall my name, ever! I may as well stay at my home and never show my face to anyone, ever! I had been asked by two people if I wouldn't mind that they stayed in my Inn for the night. I, of course, decided there was just no room: on second thought 'maybe I should have let them stay'. It was not impossible, after all; there were plenty of rooms. Then, a little while later, I decided to take a walk."

Samuel and Bartoloméo, both questioned him at the same time, "Where did you go?"

"I'm not sure, exactly. I just decided to go wherever my feet would take me, which I must admit was not too intelligent." He let out more tears, which really reminded Bartoloméo of his younger brother.

Giovanni noticed the frustration on his best friend's face, and trying to be the peacemaker said, "I'm sure he doesn't mean anything."

"True, but I don't know that he doesn't know." In all fairness, Bartoloméo only became somewhat agitated. He really had learned the art of self-mastery on this particular voyage. Then again, Beneton had no idea as to why Giovanni would say that, so he just decided to forget it. No more was said, which made Bartoloméo extremely happy.

Beneton continued, "I walked for a while. I was completely lost in the world. My mind just couldn't grasp the fact that I could have let them stay. I would have done anything to have been able to go back in time and redo the events of that night. I couldn't sleep at all, though I had sold out my place. I became lost in this world, but I was found by a heavenly light." He started to show himself for that which he wanted to become: oblivious and forgotten to the world. He was so ashamed. "If you ever get the chance, let Him in!" It was clear that Beneton felt that all was lost. The only thing he failed to realize was that he was a son of God, and therefore he had to have chosen Jesus Christ as his Redeemer and Savior at one time. Having chosen Christ's plan for him, he wasn't lost. He would, however, have to pay a certain price for the sin. Bartoloméo and his traveling companions were almost positive that the innkeeper—as he came to be known—wasn't guilty of any malicious sins, but still there would be consequences. As to the gravity of these consequences, is there anyone who will make a better judge than Christ Himself?

Everyone in the group wanted Beneton to continue, even though his breath reeked of alcohol. They knew there are more important things in life than the smell of another's breath.

"This light that I saw was so miraculous and beautiful. I don't think there's any other light that can be its equal." The alcohol definitely began to take over his speech. He started to become more and more obnoxious. It was hard for the group to keep a straight face. He was really struggling to get the words right and be taken seriously. "I was so selfish, and in one of my states of mind, I just wanted to kill myself and end it all right there and then! Then I had this vision open up to my mind. I was—what's the word?

I was like a big, overgrown, selfish child again. I just had to have everything go my way. I couldn't share a single thing. I had the worst temper as a child. I wanted everything I saw, and that ten times over. I looked up and saw a bright star. Was it ever beautiful! And it was right over my stables. 'I love it!' I exclaimed, with sheer joy in my voice! And oh, the joy! The peace I felt! Wonder and amazement filled my whole being! I can't say enough!"

An engrossed group, it seems, in unison said, "Who can?"

"Yeah, I'd like to know the same! In fact, I'd like to wager my own life that no one possesses the knowledge they need in order to be saved without His help," said the glossy-eyed innkeeper, still just a few inches away from their olfactory senses.

"You have to be pretty confident about betting your own life," said a completely mesmerized Giovanni.

"Oh, but I am! How can I doubt any more!" He went off into his own little world. "I'm just worried that I won't be able to make it, because I'm too weak to keep the commandments. As you can see, I'm not even strong enough to remain sober! I started drinking the next day. I told myself I probably should stop. But, can't you see, I'm just too weak? I'm sure that He doesn't want His kingdom to be full of drunks."

"This is all fine and good," said a truly penitent Yasser, who had been brought down to the depths of humility by what Bartoloméo had told him about being humble. "Salvation is free to all mankind, it's true, but exaltation is a different story. It must be earned! You've got to be strong! You can't just *think* you're doing what's right. But if God, himself, were to tell you to be strong: would you?" At these words, the innkeeper nodded his head in agreement. "That's partly why we are here," Yasser continued, "so we can give Him glory. But we need to know where He is. And here's a great opportunity for you to make yourself 'square' with the Father of us all! Now, if you'll be so kind as to tell us where the king lives, we'll get out of your hair."

The innkeeper slammed himself against the hard ground. Bartoloméo wondered why, because he had never seen repentance like this, before. He had to laugh. In fact, they all got quite a chuckle! This was a completely new experience, and they didn't mean to offend, but they fared much better when they laughed. The innkeeper turned himself around, thanks to Giovanni's help, and pointed to a castle that was not too far off in the distance. "There you should find him, and he should be able to tell you where the end of your quest is. I wish you well and a safe journey back to your homelands," he said, waving goodbye.

CHAPTER 22

As they walked away from the innkeeper, this thought crossed Giovanni's mind: *I wonder if we would be able to see that which was spoken of by more than just Samuel? I wonder who, besides me, is willing to stick around and see the actual Atonement? I wonder, who else is needed at home. Oh come on, Giovanni,* he told himself, *you're just going insane. No one here would be willing to stay, would they?* He looked at the others, because he thought that maybe someone from the group had heard him. Was he just going insane? Giovanni was almost certain he had heard a voice. In fact, he would have bet anything, but he was still unsure of himself—unsure that God would use him to be a leader. He needed a large boost of self-confidence, even more than Bartoloméo could give.

Giovanni tried to put on a brave face so the others would suspect he knew what he was doing, but when it came right down to it, he didn't. He was afraid that perhaps they would see his weaknesses. Excepting the Savior Himself, a true friend wouldn't mean to lead them down a "road less traveled." However, and luckily for him, the entire group had heard Beneton's words, so they had an idea of where the king lived.

They saw a large castle to their right, which seemed to them a bit extravagant. "Let's check it out!" cried an overjoyed Giovanni, who at this point really couldn't care if he was leading or following.

To Yasser, who was the wealthiest by far, it seemed a bit too much. "But what can I do? I have no way of showing anyone exactly how much wealth we have accumulated during the many years our societies have been separated from each other."

"I know what you mean," said Samuel, who was just dying to tell everyone that his people were wealthier than they were given credit. "I, personally, would give my right arm to be able to flaunt how well off we are!"

"Hey now," said an extremely honorable and humble Bartoloméo. "Just because we're rich doesn't give us the right to flaunt it."

"I very much agree with Bartoloméo," chimed in Giovanni, who was trying to be extra cool. "I don't see a reason, even the smallest hint of a reason to start fighting amongst ourselves. I think when all is said and done, we will all look back on this and be so content we came… and," he looked off into the distance, while retaining these words to himself: "at least, I hope we can."

Samuel, whose back was toward Giovanni, turned around to face him (just because one was a leader didn't mean he walked in front of the others). "It seems to me," Samuel said, "that no one has been curious to know your opinion. No one at all!" He said that in such a way as to offend. At this point, they had all been in such close proximity for so long: they had become best friends, and worst enemies.

Bartoloméo could tell—no, he knew—that something just wasn't right between the two of them. Taking one step forward, he placed himself in harm's way so neither one dared oppose him, "Does it do me good to see the two of you, who should be friends, going at each other's throats like this?" He looked somewhat lonely as he said this, but he also felt he had received much-needed strength. He was starting to feel tired again at trying to be the peacemaker, for everyone in the group would go to him with their problems; he really didn't appreciate it. But what else could he do? Everyone looked up to him, both figuratively and literally. "I'll answer that question myself: No! It doesn't do me a bit of good! We have traveled so far, and it has been so dangerous at times. I have felt the need to depend on you for food, Samuel, and on your eyes, Giovanni. But, rather than chastise you both for getting at each other's throats," he said with a smile, "and permanently causing one of you to stop functioning, as far as your lungs are concerned. If anyone at all needs to do some penance, because we are so close to our goal: it's the two of you!"

"Now?" asked a puzzled Samuel. Why he chose now to be more vocal was a mystery to all.

"Yes! Now!" replied an even more frustrated Bartoloméo. Mad wouldn't begin to describe the way he felt, and he didn't like being this way, for he preferred to be just one of the guys. It was, however, very difficult due to his size. Far too many people were afraid of him.

Being so close to their final destination, coupled with the fact that they should have been best friends because they knew each other that well, made Yasser become a completely different person. Whereas before, he was a peace-loving, docile individual—it was rare to see him any other way—he suddenly became a man with a temper. A man with a temper was bad enough, but with the added knowledge of the martial arts, he was lethal. "I think it's time to stop 'and smell the roses.' we need to be more… as one:

that is, of course, if you want to continue breathing, if not, I suggest you keep on arguing, and see where that gets you!"

Yasser had on his face, a not-so-friendly look. He, too, was disappointed in the events of the past few days. Ever since it was discovered that he spoke Aramaic, the others felt somewhat embarrassed. If they had known, they could have avoided many embarrassing situations and communicated without the help of Samuel's interpretations. This caused Samuel to be embarrassed beyond degree—almost as if he didn't want to face the others anymore. He may have been closer to Yasser than anyone else in the group, and maybe he should have known, but that was no excuse. Yasser was fed up with their self pity: "Of course if you want to end up like our friend Beneton, then by all means, keep up this act!" He proceeded to threaten them some more, until he finally was able to get their attention.

"Sorry, Yasser," came the reply from everyone, including the one who didn't really need to humble himself: Bartoloméo. For he had maintained a certain calmness and quietness throughout this entire ordeal. However, he feared no one, with the exception of maybe Yasser. It was, on the other hand, more of a respect for Yasser's ability.

"That's quite all right, my fellow travelers. Now, let's find out from the king, where exactly the Newborn Savior can be found."

CHAPTER 23

As they neared the palace (they thought it best to keep their judgments to themselves) they saw a large man sitting on an even larger throne. The thought crossed each of their minds, *Wow, this guy could be Bartoloméo's twin.* This did not make Bartoloméo happy because he felt the king just a little too soft on keeping himself in shape. It was easy for him, as it is for us all, to be a judge. Especially when it comes to unrighteous judgment. There isn't a single person who isn't guilty. The only exception: the Savior Himself!

For a more accurate account of the events, the reader is encouraged to search the scriptures, and yes, even to put any questions you may happen to have to the Bible itself: "Now when Jesus was born in Bethlehem of Judea in the days of Herod the king, behold, there came wise men from the east to Jerusalem, saying, Where is he that is born King of the Jews? For we have seen his star in the East, and are come to worship him. When Herod the king had heard these things, he was troubled, and all Jerusalem with him. And when he had gathered all the chief priests and scribes of the people together, he demanded of them where Christ should be born. And they said unto him, In Bethlehem of Judea: for thus is it written by the Prophet, And thou Bethlehem, in the land of Juda, art not the least among the princes of Juda: for out of thee shall come a Governor, that shall rule my people Israel. Then Herod, when he had privily called the wise men, enquired of them diligently what time the star appeared. And he sent them to Bethlehem, and said, Go and search diligently for the young child; and when ye have found him, bring me word again, that I may come and worship him also."

Based on what they were told, Bartoloméo and his companions had no way of knowing Herod's heart and that he actually wanted to harm Jesus. However, they were very glad to have gotten this much-needed information.

Two of them had serious doubts as to whether or not Herod had told them the truth. He said it in such a way as to make them seriously consider his words. "I don't trust the man," said a very guarded Yasser. "He just didn't seem all too honest with us."

"I know what you mean," replied an even more skeptical Samuel. "Did you see the way he looked at us? It was almost as if he didn't want us to find Him. Or that maybe he wants us to find the Child, but then perhaps he wishes to hurt Him in some way."

"I didn't notice. Sorry," said Bartoloméo. He was far too trusting of an individual to ever doubt anyone's words. Besides, he was the instigator of this particular voyage, and therefore had to be trusting. At least, he viewed his life in this way, but he was suddenly unsure of himself. "Should I have noticed? Once again, I'm sorry if I didn't notice something I should have."

From behind, a voice rang out. It was Giovanni, and he was sorry to not have come to his best friend's aid sooner. "I didn't notice either, Bartoloméo. So don't feel so bad." After a few moments, he thought he would offer more words of advice, even if these words weren't solicited. "We can all make mistakes, right Samuel?"

A resounding, "I suppose you're right!" came from ahead of them.

"Nice to see the two of you are getting along, finally," said Bartoloméo, as he put one of his 'tree trunks' around Giovanni's shoulder. This made Giovanni feel accepted, but it did not put him on speaking terms, by any stretch of the imagination, with Samuel. For still he felt they were at odds, but now it was more of a respecting each other rather than true friendship.

They continued to follow the star. They had only stopped at Herod's to make sure it was okay they were in Jerusalem. They weren't exactly sure where they should go. It's like being in an unfamiliar territory and not knowing a single thing about the customs or layout of the land. They pressed on anyway. They decided that they would just forge ahead, no matter the circumstances.

They arrived at the place Herod had told them and were greeted by two people: Mary and Joseph. They both needed absolutely no introductions whatsoever. Bartoloméo and his group had tried so hard to find them that they felt they had already known them intimately. And after presenting them the various treasures they had brought—gold, frankincense, and myrrh—Bartoloméo said, "We should probably tell you both, we hope He'll fulfill His mission."

On behalf of Bartoloméo, Yasser's face turned a bright shade of violet. He leaned closer and with a hush said, "Psst, Bartoloméo!" He then proceeded to whisper something in his ear.

After a long, shameful pause, and realizing about Whom he was speaking, Bartoloméo added, "We are sure He *will* fulfill His mission." But the doubts still seemed to take hold of Bartoloméo. Nothing like this had ever been seen or even discussed. As far as they were concerned, when a man died that was it. Therefore, he couldn't be blamed. But there is one thing that cannot be denied: he had a strong faith that no one could or dared dispute! "My apologies. He is, after all, the Creator, God, our Maker, the One, the Great Jehovah." He continued to wax poetic by giving Him all sorts of accolades, until even he realized that he was just saying the words to be heard by the other people in his group. Turning toward them he said, "My apologies. Forgive me? I don't always want to give you the impression that I'm a know it all!" Even though, he secretly wanted to be *the* big shot, especially in front of the parents of the Savior, he just felt the need to be accepted, validated.

As each one presented their gifts, and all Mary could say in return was "Thanks," they wondered why she had chosen to maintain silence during their visit. It was a mystery.

Later that night, when Joseph would question her as to why she had chosen to keep silent as gifts were presented to them both, she said, "You are right. You don't need to remind me that I wasn't friendly. I'd just like to see them give up something *they* love for the sake of following Him. I'd like to see them give up something for the word's sake! I know not why I was chosen to be the mother of the Son of God. I sometimes wonder why no one else could have done the job better than I. People will always have their doubts, especially of Him!" She went off on this dialogue until she was blue in the face. She had no other way to vent her frustration. Only, she was as calm as one could be! "I'd like to wager anything that" (here, again, the self-doubts began to make themselves a large a part of her life) "—however strange it may seem—I will be seen as something far greater than my Son Himself in some parts of the world. I wish there were some way to go forward in time and get everyone to believe the way they should!" Her desire was that everyone believed in her Son as the Redeemer. She just couldn't understand why anyone would want to worship her and not the Savior Himself! *After all, He is the one*—she told herself—*who will die for us, is He not?*

While it may be true that she was special, Mary still didn't possess any "godlike qualities" that so many people now believe her to have. A simple reading of the Bible will allow you to know that you cannot "make unto you (these) graven images."

CHAPTER 24

That same night, Giovanni had a dream (more like a nightmare) that they shouldn't return to Herod. Although wanting to go back, he said to the others, "I don't think we should return. I think that Herod will kill the Child! Maybe, that is why we should do as Samuel and Yasser suggest and not return!" He had also thought to have seen many friends from their hometown, "now, what do they want... don't they know we're already here!" He couldn't see, or recognize the changing of his ailment. "They could have just come with us, there is no need to bring a totally different mode of transportation. Sure," he started to smile, "they could have stayed cooped up with us, and maybe Samuel and I wouldn't be arguing so much. They could have taken the brunt of our 'little war'."

Bartoloméo had noticed Giovanni's eyes now were giving out on him, "What's wrong with my best friend? Now, who needs his mommy!"

Giovanni didn't become irate, even though he had every right to do so. No, he too, was too humble to allow things to get out of control. "I do. I'll admit that I shouldn't repeat myself as often as I do. So sorry. Is there anything I could do to make it up to the group?" He was always sorry for something. He didn't know what, but he felt that he should apologize all the same.

This time, Samuel came to his rescue: "It's okay." He placed an arm around Giovanni's shoulder. "It happens to the best of us." From that moment on, Giovanni knew he had a friend for life. So the thing between them actually became a good thing.

Speaking to his now latest friend, Giovanni gave him a nod of the head. "Thanks! I needed that more than anyone knows."

"Don't mention it. Some of us have to stick together." He gave Giovanni a quick wink of the eye, then told him just how valuable he was.

This caused Bartoloméo to smile on the inside. Some boys just knew how to resolve their differences, and some didn't. He continued to think, I wish the world could see how we could all resolve the differences between us. Then he suddenly found himself going off in his own little world. "I wish I were an angel and had the power to shake the earth with just my voice." He started to think of his brother and wound up breaking his own unspoken rule. "I wish Philipiano were here. Maybe then, and only then, would he be able to see what the faithful can do! But as it turns out, he stayed home 'to take care of dad,' who in my opinion, should have come along as well, but didn't. Why is it I was born into such a non-believing and faithless family? I bet that even mom, with her faith, wouldn't be able to convince them otherwise."

We can't always see what the future holds. But if you have the faith of a child, you can do unspeakable things. However, if we lack the necessary faith, then what do we do? We can trust. After all, isn't that what faith is? He, who has all power, wants us to trust in Him.

By trusting in Him, you won't have any desire to take advantage of your fellow man. You won't lie, cheat, steal, or do any drugs. You will love your neighbor as you do yourself. You won't try to take advantage of someone else because he may or may not have said something—even if the "something" he said works out in your favor.

Made in the USA
San Bernardino, CA
26 December 2014